Leap of
FAITH

More from the FAITH series

HAVE A LITTLE FAITH
KEEP THE FAITH

Other books by Candy Harper

THE STRAWBERRY SISTERS: PERFECTLY ELLA

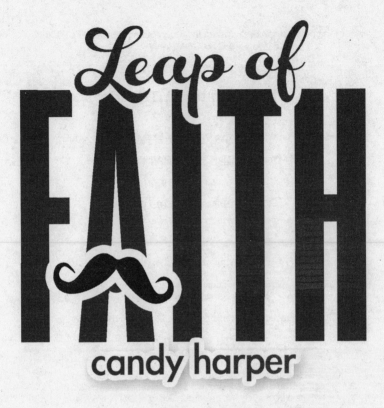

Leap of FAITH

candy harper

SIMON & SCHUSTER

First published in Great Britain in 2015 by Simon & Schuster UK Ltd
A CBS COMPANY

1 3 5 7 9 10 8 6 4 2

Simon & Schuster UK Ltd
1st Floor, 222 Gray's Inn Road
London
WC1X 8HB

www.simonandschuster.co.uk

Simon & Schuster Australia, Sydney
Simon & Schuster India, New Delhi

A CIP catalogue record for this book is available from the British Library.

PB ISBN 978-1-47112-419-8
eBook ISBN 978-1-47112-420-4

Typeset in the UK by M Rules
Printed and bound by CPI Group (UK) Ltd, Croydon, CR0 4YY

MIX
Paper from
responsible sources
FSC® C020471

Simon & Schuster UK Ltd are committed to sourcing paper that is made from
wood grown in sustainable forests and supports the Forest Stewardship
Council, the leading international forest certification organisation. Our
books displaying the FSC logo are printed on FSC certified paper.

For Chessie

APRIL

FRIDAY 20TH APRIL

I haven't had a very good Easter holiday. It's hard to hop about like a happy bunny when the boy you like has started seeing someone else.

Megs rang me this morning. I can always rely on my best friend to bring sunshine and cheerfulness into my life, even when the universe is punishing me. When I picked up the phone she said, 'Are you still moping, you great turnip?'

'You're such a comfort to me, Megs.'

'All I'm saying is you can't keep worrying about what could have been with Ethan if you hadn't been such a stupid-pants. Just because you've made a huge mistake letting him think you're not interested, and now he's seeing gorgeous Dawn, you can't spend every minute thinking about what a massive potato you are.'

'I'm not! I've done lots of things this holiday that haven't involved thinking about Ethan.'

'Like what?'

'Insulting my little brother and eating my own weight in Easter eggs.'

'That's marvellous. Maybe next week you could try for a smile.'

'I don't feel like smiling,' I said. 'How about laying some blame? I think I've got the energy for that. I'll keep it simple: Megan, I blame you for everything that is wrong in my life.'

'I see,' Megs replied. 'Is this the usual blame that I get for the biscuits running out, and you forgetting that you're not allowed to sing rude songs about Mr Hampton while we're actually in one of his lessons? Or have you found a new and ridiculous way to pin everything on me?'

'It was you who said I should go out with Ethan in the first place.'

'And I was right! You two are perfectly suited.'

'Someone seems to have forgotten to mention that to Queen of the Night, Dawn.'

'If you hadn't wasted time hanging out with pretty-boy Finn, none of this would have happened. Ethan couldn't wait around forever.'

I knew it was true but none of this was making me feel any better.

'I just wish he'd waited another hour, I was going to tell him I like him.'

Megs sighed. 'Don't worry; it won't last between him and Dawn.'

'Really?'

'Yeah, the rate I've seen them snogging at they'll have worn their lips out by half term.'

Brilliant.

LATER

I might just forget about boys for a while. This is going to be a busy term, you know, with mock exams to sit, teachers to wind up and science labs to set on fire. I'm already going to have to work pretty hard if I want to keep up my commitment to spending several hours a day lounging about, eating biscuits.

Besides, my track record with boys really isn't great. My first boyfriend, Finn, was super sweet and delicious looking, but it turns out that while that scores full marks in a cupcake, you need a bit more in a boyfriend. Then I realised how smart and funny and good looking Ethan is. Unfortunately, just as I discovered this, he discovered the inside of Dawn's mouth, and apparently he liked it because he's been spending a lot of time in there recently.

But despite Megs comparing me to all the least flattering vegetables, I am not completely miserable. There's more to life than boys.

Maybe I'll concentrate on being a good friend for a while.

SATURDAY 21ST APRIL

Megs and I went round to our friend Westy's house.

Westy is six foot tall with shoulders to match, but he is ninety-six per cent giant teddy bear, and he always makes me laugh. He also has the sort of considerate parents that go away for a wedding and leave him and his big brother to conduct their business in peace. Although, Westy doesn't exactly do peace; something is always making a loud rumbling sound, his drum kit, his stomach or a bunch of angry people following him, wanting to ask about their trampled flowers or broken fences. But he never means to upset anyone. You can't help liking Westy.

When Megs and I arrived, Megs's boyfriend, Cameron, was already there.

'Faith! Megan!' Westy said as if he was really surprised to see us, even though he'd only invited us round half an hour ago. Then he actually managed to pick us both up at the same time and shake us about a bit. It's not a good idea to visit Westy straight after you've eaten.

Cameron managed to wave at me before he attached himself to Megs' face. They got down to some seriously squelchy snogging. I hope I don't sound like I'm gargling with yoghurt when I kiss.

'Lot of couples at the moment,' Westy said. He was watching Megs and Cam like they were fish in a tank. Snoggy fish. 'You ever think about getting another boyfriend, Faith?'

I didn't want to tell Westy that actually I've got a thing for Ethan so I just said, 'I'm happy as I am for now.'

Westy looked thoughtful. 'So ... you're not seeing anyone at the moment?'

'Nope.' Now that I'd started thinking about Ethan I couldn't stop. I wondered if he was out with

Dawn. 'Anybody else coming round?' I asked Westy in a very laid-back and casual way.

'I rang everybody,' Westy said. 'Lily didn't answer her phone.'

'She's gone to see Arif,' I said. 'She's spent most of the holidays on the train going to visit him. It's a miracle she hasn't ended up in Edinburgh.'

'That is lucky,' he sucked his teeth like a disapproving old man. Compared to Lily, Westy seems quite sane and stable. 'And Angharad is at the library.'

I nodded. I've long suspected that, unlike the rest of us, Angharad doesn't watch TV or sleep, she just fuels up at libraries and museums.

'Eliot says he's got homework to do.'

We both pulled a face.

'But Ethan said he'd come.'

'Oh.' I wasn't sure what I thought about that. I hadn't seen him since I had a ringside seat for his big kiss with Dawn.

Megs opened one eye, mid-snog, to exchange a look with me. While I admire her multi-tasking, it was fairly disgusting. Still it was quite a sympathetic one-eyed, mid-slurp look, so I'll forgive her.

Westy got tired of watching Megs and Cam and decided to show me his collection of fake body parts. He particularly enjoyed modelling some massive fake ears with droopy lobes. 'I look just like my

Grandad,' he said. 'Do you want to see my severed head?'

'Of course.'

'I'll go and get it. My mum's a bit funny about me leaving it lying around. Once, she dialled two nines before she realised it was Reginald.'

'Reginald?'

'Yeah, that's his name.'

So he'd just scooted upstairs to fetch his rubber head friend when the doorbell rang. Megs had the good grace to stop chomping at Cameron to say, 'I'll get it.'

I shook my hair back and tried to look like I didn't fancy anyone. Or if I did that it was someone very charismatic and rich who fancied me right back.

I heard the door open.

'Oh,' Megs said really loudly. 'Hi *Ethan*, and this must be your friend *Dawn*.'

I think this was Megs's subtle attempt to give me time to prepare for the fact that Ethan had brought his new girlfriend along. I don't know what she thought I was going to do in the seven seconds I had before they appeared in the room. Climb out the cat flap? I mean I may have exited through a kitchen window once before, but if your so-called friends barricade you in the kitchen at a party when you've drunk too much Sprite, there's either the sink or the back garden.

Anyway, I wasn't sure what the cat flap / kitchen window situation was so instead I just sat there.

I wanted to give the impression that I really didn't care, that I was totally relaxed and completely cool with everything. I leant back and lowered my eyelids. Just as the sitting room door was opening Cameron nudged me, 'Are you nodding off?'

I jerked forward in what I can only hope was an attractive fashion.

Ethan and Dawn were right there in front of me.

Holding hands.

Looking attractive and happy.

Honestly, some people have got no idea of the polite way to behave when they're a guest in someone's house.

'Hi Faith,' Ethan said. 'You know Dawn, right?'

I smiled. 'Hey, Dawn.' I had to concentrate quite hard to not call her Yawn or Spawn or any of the other hilarious names I've thought of for her. 'I've seen you around. You were at the club night at our school, weren't you?'

She smiled back. Hers was the proper kind that you actually mean. 'Yeah, and I kind of gate-crashed your birthday party a bit! Hope you didn't mind.'

'No, course not.' For once I was grateful that my runaway mouth was saying the exact opposite to what I was thinking. I wondered if it was at my party that Dawn and Ethan started getting friendly.

Ethan turned round. 'And you know Cam.'

Cam grinned.

'And you may remember Megan from such events as The Party We Just Talked About and the whole Opening The Door Thing.'

Megs gave her a pretty chilly nod. She was being offish for my sake. She's a good friend.

'And I'm Westy,' said Westy, coming back into the room. He stuck out his hand but there was a rubber head on it. Everyone looked at the head.

'And this is Reginald,' Westy said.

'That's a nice head,' Dawn said.

Westy beamed at her.

The happy couple sat down on the sofa. 'Cam is Megan's boyfriend,' Ethan explained to Dawn.

'That's what Megs's Grammy calls me. Isn't it Megs? She can't remember my name so she says "Megan's young man! Wash those cups up! Megan's boy! Are you going to help your girlfriend on with her coat, or did your mother never teach you manners?"'

'It'll make things easier when Megan replaces you,' Ethan said.

We all laughed, except Cam who punched Ethan on the arm.

'You do get introduced like that a lot though, don't you Cam?' I said. 'To Megs's millions of cousins and when we go to parties and that. Are you tired of being defined in terms of Megan? Do you feel like footballers' girlfriends do – like you've got no identity of your own? Like you're just "Megan's boyfriend"?'

Cameron stared at me, then looked at Megan. 'But I am her boyfriend.'

'Yeah, but Megs is the more famous one of you two isn't she? People know who Megs is. Do you feel diminished?'

Cameron pulled a face. 'Well, I didn't used to.'

Dawn laughed. 'Maybe you should ask Megan for an allowance, Cam. You know, to spend on diamonds and high heels.'

Ethan smiled at her. I started wishing I'd crawled out of the cat flap when I had the chance.

'I don't wear girls' shoes!' Cam was getting a bit worked up.

Megs patted him on the knee. 'They're taking the micky.'

'Yeah, well …' Cam scowled. 'Westy dressed up like a girl in drama once!'

Westy nodded Reginald in agreement. 'I'm quite good at plaits,' he said proudly.

The conversation ground to a halt there and we all stared at each other.

'So you'll be able to get in some drum practice while your parents are away,' Ethan said to Westy.

'Yep, I've been working on a new song. It's called "Killer Custard Cream".'

'Sounds good. Dawn plays the drums.'

'Cool,' I said. The fact that I meant it made me feel a bit droopy. I wasn't sure I wanted to hear any more of Dawn's accomplishments so I said, 'Can we have a cup of tea, Westy?'

'Yeah, course.' He got up.

'I'll help you,' I said.

The kitchen was very untidy. Every surface was covered with used plates and cups. Dirty saucepans and a frying pan were stacked on the cooker.

'You need to do a bit of washing up,' I said.

'Yep, I don't think anyone's done it since my parents left.'

'When did they leave?'

Westy squinted a bit. 'It's Saturday today, isn't it?'

'Yes. So how long have they been gone?'

'About an hour and a half.'

'What on earth? How have you managed to make all this mess in that time?'

'It was my brother's idea. A load of his mates turned up and he said we should have a fry up.'

'Let's have a cup of tea and then maybe I can help you sort it out.'

It was a job to get the kettle under the tap because the sink was so full of plates but I managed to fill it.

'Cups ... cups ...' Westy said. He looked

helplessly around the kitchen and started yanking open cupboard doors.

'Doesn't have to be bone china,' I said. 'Anything will do.'

He opened a drawer. 'I can offer you a ladle or an egg cup.'

He was starting to pink up with embarrassment, so I said, 'Let's just rinse a few of these out, shall we?'

But the group of mugs on the counter were full of some sort of tar like substance and several of them had what looked like fish scales floating in them. So I emptied out the sink and gave them a proper scrub.

Eventually we had six cups of tea to take back to the sitting room.

'You took your time,' Megs said. 'What were you two doing out there?'

Dawn looked from me to Westy.

Westy turned pink. I attempted to discretely strangle Megan with her own legs. There was a bit of a tussle and Megs said, 'Cam! Do something!'

Cam blinked in surprise. I'm not sure he'd noticed that Megs and I were wrestling. 'Stop cuddling my girlfriend, Faith.'

I gave her one last Chinese burn and let her go. But only because my tea was getting cold.

Cam seemed worn out by his misguided attempts to please Megs. He flopped back in his chair and said, 'I'm hungry. Westy, can I have something to eat?'

'Sure. Help yourself.'

Cam went to the kitchen and we talked about going back to school. Dawn said her school is really strict. I told her that if their head evil dictator ever needs replacing they could have Miss Ramsbottom for no charge.

Cam reappeared eating cereal out of a teapot with a medicine spoon.

'If we're going to get to the cinema in time we should probably leave now,' Ethan said to Dawn.

I decided to study Reginald's alarming eyebrows as a distraction.

'It was nice to meet you all,' Dawn said. And off they went. Holding hands again in a totally unnecessary fashion.

I exhaled.

Westy came back from seeing them out. 'What did you think of Dawn?' he asked.

Megs screwed up her nose in an unimpressed fashion.

Cam shrugged.

'Yeah,' said Westy. 'She was a bit quiet. I like my girls loud.'

'They'd have to be loud to get a word in edgeways,' Cam said.

But the horrible truth about Dawn is that she is

not an awful person. She wasn't a bit unpleasant. She didn't even smell bad.

She and Ethan will probably have dark-haired, twinkly-eyed, delightfully sarcastic children together.

SUNDAY 22ND APRIL

School starts again tomorrow. Seriously. Again. It just keeps coming round. I complained about this to Mum.

'It's like the circle of life, isn't it?' she said.

This is typical of my mother's misguided hippy nonsense.

'It's not at all like the circle of life,' I said. 'They're completely different things. The circle of life is one lion dying and another lion becoming king.' I poked her to make sure she was listening. 'The circle of life is what you say to old people to try and make them feel better about their imminent death. It's got nothing to do with school. School is more like that big round rock in Indiana Jones, the one that chases you out whichever way you turn and won't go away.'

'I wish you'd view your education as an opportunity rather than a punishment.'

'And I wish that the royal family would reveal that they'd just discovered an evil chamber maid switched me with your real daughter at birth. You've got to manage your expectations, Mum.'

Then she threatened to manage me by cutting off my pocket money so I gave up on trying to explain the drudgery of my life to her.

MONDAY 23RD APRIL

There is no doubt that school is a criminal waste of my time and talent, and the teachers are clearly sadists who have failed at real life and have returned to the comforting environment of their youth, (which smells of gym mats and school dinners and sweaty changing rooms and Icky Vicky Blundell's insect repellent perfume) so they can boss about poor defenceless teenagers in order to pretend that they are in control of something.

Still, it is quite a nice place for a chat with your friends.

In between the suffering and the mental torture and all that.

LATER

Speaking of suffering and torture I bumped into Icky on my way to registration. I say bumped into, but actually she crossed three lanes of fast moving girl-traffic in order to deliberately crash into me.

'Hold on, Vicky,' I said. 'I appreciate you're desperate to smother me in affection, but if you really want a cuddle, you're going to have to get in line behind my family, friends and several dozen fit boys.'

'Yeah, right,' she sneered. 'As if you could get someone hot anywhere near you. Finn legged it as soon as he could, didn't he?'

'Actually, I think you'll find that I ended that relationship.'

She gave me a sceptical look. I showed what a noble person I am by refraining from walloping her.

'Can't handle the truth, can you?' she said screwing up her evil button nose. 'Don't worry I've told everyone for you. Everybody in this school and at Radcliffe knows that Finn dumped you because you smell of rotten fish.'

What a cow. I split up with Finn weeks ago, but Icky obviously can't deal with the fact that an attractive boy really liked me, so she carries on spreading her horrible lies. I held my punching arm tight to my side.

'Ah,' I said, forcing a smile. 'Poor little Vicky, my pity for you is so strong that I am going to let you in on something special. Really, your mother should have shared this with you, but I imagine it's hard for her to look at your spiteful monkey face without weeping, as she realises that her hopes of having a daughter who isn't filled with hate and rage and bad taste in cheap jewellery are dead now. But I'll tell you the secret . . .'

I leaned in close and even though Icky was glowering at me she couldn't help instinctively moving a little nearer.

'If you're constantly thinking you can smell rotten fish,' I whispered. 'Then it's time to have a bath.'

And I sped off before she started shooting out shrill squeals like a very angry firework.

I arrived at our tutor room hoping for a more relaxing chat, but what I got was Lily saying, 'They're not going to run out of Marmite, are they?'

And I realised that what I'd missed over Easter was a daily dose of Lily silliness.

I put down my bag. 'Don't worry, last time I checked the shops had plenty of Marmite.'

She frowned. 'Yes, but how long will it last? I mean where does it come from? And what happens when they've dug it all out?'

I snorted. 'They don't mine Marmite. They make it.'

'What from?'

'Er, yeast I think.'

'And how much yeast have we got?'

'Enough.' But I could tell just from the look on her face that she was planning a secret underground Marmite store. If there is ever a global disaster, I'm heading to Lily's for snacks.

Then Angharad arrived and I thought that

things might take a more sane turn, but Angharad has got her own worries.

She showed us a file of the revision that she's done this holiday.

'The mocks aren't for weeks,' I said.

'I know, but I've got a lot going on this term; I'm captain of the netball team and I've signed up to help Year Sevens who are struggling with their maths. So I need to be super organised.'

'You'll be fine, Ang,' Lily said, drawing a diagram of some sort of bunker all over Ang's notes.

Ang wrinkled her nose. 'Am I worrying too much?'

I didn't want her to start worrying about worrying so I changed the subject. 'Did you see Elliot in the holidays?'

Elliot is just as hardworking (and tiny) as Angharad.

She smiled shyly. 'A couple of times. We did some Physics revision together.'

Lily fanned herself. 'Nothing hotter than Physics.'

'It was quite exciting,' Ang agreed.

I had to wait until English to get any really sensible conversation. Then Megs and I were able to have an in depth discussion on the best way to eat a cupcake without the icing going up your nose.

My mum is right: school really is quite thought provoking.

TUESDAY 24TH APRIL

Mum insisted that I help her feel less alone in her pointless existence by hanging out with her in the kitchen, chopping vegetables for dinner. Then she put on her serious face and said, 'Faith, I've got something to tell you and I need you to not have a tantrum.'

'You're not going to wear those knee boots again, are you?'

She passed me a carrot. 'No. Although there's no reason why a woman of my age can't wear boots.'

'I can think of two reasons: your left leg and your right one.'

'I'm trying to tell you something, Faith.'

My heart plummeted. 'You're not sending me to boarding school are you?'

'No Faith, it's—'

'Are you sending Sam to boarding school? Because I've got to say that would be less of a tantrum situation and more of a skippy dance time.'

'Why don't you just listen and find out?'

'Because you've just told me not to have a tantrum, so now I'm imagining all my worst fears coming true.'

Mum took a deep breath. 'Next month, Granny is coming to stay with us.'

I nearly sliced my finger off. 'Oh. Well. That's not my worst fear.'

'Good.'

'That's Armageddon.'

Mum shook her head. 'Don't exaggerate.'

'Granny-geddon.'

'That's not a thing.'

I narrowed my eyes. 'Let's see what you say after she's been here for a few days.'

Mum attacked some green beans. 'I'm sure it will be fine.'

'Where's she going to sleep? I know she looks like a shrivelled old fruit bat, but I don't think she actually hangs from the rafters at night.'

She gave me a sheepish look, which is usually a good indication that she has done something truly awful.

'Not in my room?'

'It's bigger than Sam's. You can sleep on the pull-out sofa in the dining room.'

Unbelievable. 'Listen Mum, I don't know why you've chosen to tell me that you've given my one place of refuge away to a grasping old woman, while I've got a sharp knife in my hand, but I suggest you start thinking about how to use that chopping board as a shield.'

She ignored that, but I noticed that she took a couple of steps backwards. 'I'm sorry Faith, but in a family sometimes you have to make sacrifices.'

I gave a massive sigh and hacked more carrots

to pieces in a quietly dignified fashion, which I think indicated that I have already made a great number of sacrifices for this family – like remaining in it.

'It's not going to be for long,' Mum said. 'A few weeks at most.'

'That's what she's told you. She's like a vampire; once you invite her in there'll be no end to the blood and violence.'

She folded her arms. 'You're going to have to tone down the cutting remarks while she's here.'

No bedroom and no insulting people. I may as well sign up to a convent. 'Why is she coming anyway?'

'Because she's having her kitchen done and she doesn't want to be there for all the drilling and paint fumes.'

'What? She breathes out poison all the time! I can't see what harm taking a bit in would do her.'

'Faith!'

'Oh, come on, there's not much time left for her lungs anyway. She may as well take up cigar smoking and pearl diving and make the most of them.'

'That's not a nice way to talk. We all know you love your granny really.'

'Yep. Really, as in really *really* deep down. Way down under several hundred feet of annoyance and irritation.'

'You'd better start drilling then because I think we're all going to need a lot of love when she arrives.'

LATER

I'm trying to put Granny's imminent invasion out of my mind and focus on the present. It's the first debating club tomorrow and I'm not sure if I'm looking forward to it or not. Ethan will be there and I'm afraid that I'm never going to be able to have a good chat with him again, because I'll always be thinking about how things might have been different.

WEDNESDAY 25TH APRIL

I do feel really proud of debating club; it's brilliant that something I started is doing so well. There were even more new recruits today. Of course, Icky was all over the Radcliffe boys. Not that I have a problem with that; obviously, the main reason we're all there is to mix with boys – and to learn the vital life-skill of arguing. But I do think nabbing six boys all to yourself is just greedy. How she persuaded one of them to give her a shoulder-carry thirty seconds after meeting him, I have no idea.

I gave the fresh talent the once over myself, you know, in a friendly way. There were a couple of quite cool looking Year Elevens, but somehow my eyes kept going back to Ethan. At least I don't have to watch him and Dawn being all hilarious and well suited. She goes to St Mildred's on the other side of town.

Actually, it wasn't as uncomfortable as I thought it might be. Ethan came over and said, 'Nice to see you ladies. I very nearly didn't make it here, there were a lot of people vying for my company tonight.'

Megs said, 'Oh yeah?'

I thought he was going to mention Spawn but he said, 'Uh huh. My form tutor, the head, the police ... all dying to have a chat with me.'

'I think you're mistaking popularity with their keenness to earn that reward that's been put up for your capture,' I said.

'That would explain why people keep trying to bundle me into cars with blacked out windows.'

'I think that's just motorists who've taken an instant dislike to you.'

He grinned. 'You excited about the new term then, Faith?'

I was starting to relax and enjoy myself. 'Oh, yes. You know me, I live for my education.'

'Goes on a bit though, doesn't it? I mean I know some slow types need it ground into them, but you'd think they'd realise that smart people like me and you had pretty much got it covered by the end of Year Eight.'

I nodded. 'Seems crazy that we've still got years

to go. I was thinking about starting one of those tally charts like prisoners scrape on the walls of their cell. Only I thought maybe I'd just smash a school window for each day.'

'That seems like an appropriate way to mark the time stolen from you. I might do a similar thing by letting down the tyres on a teacher's car each day.'

'Don't talk to me about teachers' cars.'

He cracked up. There was a bit of an unfortunate incident a while back involving Miss Ramsbottom's car and one of my stupid ideas. Ethan sort of got me out of that one.

Then it was time to listen to the debate. On the whole I feel a bit better about Ethan. I'd forgotten how much I enjoy just chatting to him. Maybe we can still be friends.

THURSDAY 26TH APRIL

While I am enjoying all this being a good friend, I thought that maybe I should be broadening my horizons. Maybe I should be making new friends ... in different countries. So I had a little chat with Mum tonight.

'Remember when I was gracious enough to inform you that I had suffered a disappointment in my personal life that you weren't allowed to ask me about, but which I also suggested meant I should get twice as much pudding as everyone else until further notice? And you were gracious enough not to spout a load of hippy 'wisdom' at me, but you did say that I shouldn't dwell on it and that I should move on to the next challenge in my life?'

'Mmm hmm.' She wrinkled up her nose in a suspicious fashion.

'Why are you wrinkling your nose in a suspicious fashion?'

'Oh, I don't know. Maybe it's because you're talking.' She pushed her straggly hippy hair out of her eyes. 'And I've had conversations with you before. The way that they've ended has taught me to begin with suspicion otherwise I wind up being bamboozled into some ridiculous plan of yours.'

'Charming.'

'Wait a second, I'll just activate my bamboozle barrier.'

And she pretended to erect some sort of force field. She's so childish. I don't know why the authorities let her keep me.

I folded my arms. 'So you admit that you're suspicious. That's nice, isn't it? When some mothers hear their child's voice they start to well up with love and pride, but you just purse your wrinkly lips and expect the worst from me. It's a wonder I haven't turned to crime.'

I thought she was going to launch into some tutting and huffing, but instead she nodded. 'You're right. I shouldn't tease when you're trying to be serious. Just wipe those negative vibes away.'

And she actually mimed wiping off an invisible blackboard like some sort of geriatric CBeebies presenter. 'Now, what did you want to say, sweetheart?'

'I need a holiday.'

'A holiday?'

'I thought somewhere educational. Like New York or Ibiza.'

Her CBeebies grin faltered. 'How are either of those locations educational?'

'Travel broadens the mind. If I went to both then my mind would be pretty broad by the time I got back.'

She was a bit of a funny colour at this point so I said, 'Actually, you look a little peaky, perhaps you should have a holiday too. Except, I know that you and Dad aren't really money-making go-getters, so perhaps it would be more sensible if you went somewhere closer to home. Maybe you could stay with Aunt Joyce?'

She opened and shut her mouth. Which I could kind of understand because at Aunt Joyce's house you're not allowed to put anything down without a mat under it, and that includes your head. Seriously, all of her pillows have got crocheted doily things on. But I had given this some thought.

'I'm suggesting Aunt Joyce's because then you'd be near enough to keep an eye on Sam.'

'Sam?'

I nodded. 'You might be called to a meeting with his head teacher, or a court appearance or something. I mean, I know you haven't bothered much with his upbringing so far, but if you're really strict from now on maybe you can avoid having him butcher us all in our beds.'

She snorted.

'Was that a snort of agreement? Or is your body protesting about your vegan lifestyle?'

She snorted again.

'Are you laughing? I thought you wanted me to take more of an interest in Sam.'

She hiccupped in a very undignified fashion. 'Oh Faith, is this really your way of asking for a holiday?'

'I prefer to call it an educational trip of a lifetime.'

'Nobody could accuse you of sucking up to get what you want like some teenagers. Although if you ever wanted to go down that route, you know there's good behaviour, washing up, foot rubs ...'

I shuddered.

'I just want you to know that your father and I are very open to that sort of bribery. Your dad would probably accept cash too.'

'Due to the fact that you've failed to provide me with a fortune to inherit I haven't got a lot of money, but if you say yes I might think about some washing up. With the exception of Sam's plates. I dread to think what you could catch from his spit.'

Mum didn't say anything.

'So you'll think about it?' I asked.

'I find myself completely unable to think about anything other than what a cheeky madam you are.'

It seems that my parents are not prepared to help me experience world culture. They would rather my brain rotted in this stifling environment. We haven't even got any paintings by famous artists and I clearly remember that the last time I tried to express myself through dance Dad got very shirty when I knocked over some horrible old ornament.

They're lucky that I'm naturally extraordinary.

FRIDAY 27TH APRIL

This morning Angharad said to me, 'Becky says they're giving out the French exchange letters this afternoon. Do you want to go?'

Well. This just goes to prove that when I told my mother I don't need to plan for the future because the universe recognises life's winners and takes care of them, I WAS RIGHT. My lazy parents aren't going to organise a holiday for me, but that's okay because I will be going on the French exchange trip. In fact, the French department are much more likely to make a decent job of it, we all know they've got plenty of time to sort out flights and a luxury hotel for me because it's not like teaching French takes much out of you, is it? In my lessons Madame Badeau mostly shouts 'Asseyez-vous, Faith!' and fans herself with a copy of Tricolore.

I beamed at Angharad. 'I'm definitely going. It'll be brilliant. And frankly, it's about time that the French department started giving back. I haven't forgotten that they still owe me an hour in bed from that time they made us come into school early to go to that ridiculous French breakfast where all we got was watered down Lidl cocoa and a sniff of a croissant. It's nice to see that they've finally started taking my needs into consideration.'

Angharad blinked. 'Oh. I thought it might be useful for vocabulary.'

Angharad is a great girl but I do sometimes worry about her ability to focus on what's important in life. 'I'll tell you what this trip is going to be useful for,' I said. 'For buying lovely things in fancy French shops and scoffing lovely cakes in fancy French patisseries and snogging lovely French boys in fancy French ... er, I'm not sure where French boys like to gather, but we're going to find out!' I squeezed her into a hug. 'We're going on holiday!'

Angharad wiggled out of my arms. 'I need to ask my mum first.'

'Yeah, of course, me too. Either that or I'm going

to have to get a lot better at forging her signature. But you do want to go, don't you?'

She was fidgeting with her bag. 'Yes … No … I don't know.'

'It'll be fun. Croissants, cheese, shopping, maybe some sightseeing.'

'That does sound nice, but what if I can't understand what people are saying?'

'You're great at French, Ang. And you can always ask them to slow down or talk English like a proper person.'

She nodded, but I could see she was still worrying.

'It will be brilliant, I promise.'

When Lily arrived, Ang asked her if she fancied the trip. I thought Lily would be up for a holiday but after she'd thought about it for a minute she shook her head.

'I don't think it's a good idea,' she said. 'People never seem to understand what I'm saying even when I'm talking English.'

She had a point there. I wasn't sure France was ready for Lily.

'And I hate packing. I always seem to end up with too many spoons and not enough glue.'

'Well, that happens to us all,' I said.

Lily nodded as if we were having an entirely sane conversation. 'I might give it a miss.'

Ang looked horribly disappointed.

'Don't worry,' I said to her. 'You'll have me and Megs to look after you.'

But when I told Megs in Physics she didn't seem that keen. I'll have to work on her.

I've been walloping Sam all night to get my bashing arm ready.

SATURDAY 28TH APRIL

I went shopping with the girls this morning. As we were coming out of Topshop I spotted Ethan and Dawn getting off a bus.

'Is that her?' Lily asked in a whisper that was louder than most people's normal voice.

'Yep,' Megs said. 'That's Spawn.'

'You've seen her before,' Angharad said. 'Remember? At the club night and Faith's birthday.'

Lily shook her head. 'I can only really remember people's heads if I talk to them. Then I can picture their face by thinking about the words coming out of their mouth.'

'Okaaay,' Megs said.

I didn't say anything; I was too busy watching Ethan put his arm around Dawn.

'She's got a very nice head,' Lily said.

'Yep,' I agreed. 'Nice head. Witty banter. Charming personality. She's pigging marvellous.'

At that moment Ethan spotted us. I hope that

spitting out the words 'Pigging marvellous' showed off my profile in its best light.

'Hey!' he called and pulled Dawn across the road to speak to us.

'Hi Ethan,' Lily said. 'What are you up to?'

'We're just heading to the Picture House, they've got this film festival, it's a bit ... arty—'

'Farty,' Dawn finished.

Hell, they're at the finishing each other's sentences stage already.

'But today is vintage horror films. Do you want to join us?'

'No thank you,' Angharad said.

Lily shook her head. 'When I watch horror films people get really annoyed with me because I keep laughing.'

'I'm broke,' Megs said.

Dawn looked at me. It wasn't even in a don't-you–dare-ruin-my-date way. She seemed perfectly happy for me to tag along, but I didn't much fancy being a gooseberry.

'I don't think I'm allowed in the Picture House,' I said. 'Last time I was there I got into a fist fight with my granny about whether I could fit the entire contents of one of these titchy pots of ice cream into my mouth at once – which I totally can, by the way. We were removed from the building.'

Dawn looked blank.

Ethan looked impressed.

It's lucky that my behaviour provides me with an excuse not to go pretty much anywhere in this town.

'I guess we'll see you then,' Ethan said and they strolled off.

We didn't stay long after that. I was a bit distracted wondering what it would be like sitting in a dark cinema with Ethan. Plus, Megs didn't have any money because her parents are saving up to send Grammy to Barbados to visit Megs's great auntie, and Ang wanted to hurry home and prepare to tutor Year Sevens in maths by making sure she's got enough squared paper or something.

It was a small comfort to me that Lily will now forever remember Spawn by picturing the word 'farty' coming out of her mouth.

LATER

When I got home, Dad insisted that I help him make lunch. So I pointed at things in the freezer that I thought I could eat without vomiting and he dribbled on about his boring life.

'Where's Mum?' I asked, which is an indication of just how boring he was because it's not like I had any actual interest in the whereabouts of old Patchouli Pants.

'She's gone to yoga with Simon.'

Simon runs the wholefood shop next door to

my mum's shop of New Age nonsense. They're each other's best customers. And despite the fact he is possibly even duller than my dad, he's the closet thing my mum has got to a friend. I looked at Dad.

'And you don't mind?'

'Mind what?'

'Mum. Being friends with Simon.'

He shrugged. 'Any friendship that gets us a discount on your mother's beansprout habit is fine in my book.'

'But you think it's possible for men and women to be friends?'

'Of course.'

'Even if one of them fancies the other one?'

'I don't think there's anything romantic between your mother and Simon.'

I'm pretty sure he's right. I can't imagine anyone fancying my mum as it is, but it would be absolutely impossible once you'd been forced to see her doing the downward dog pose in her shorts.

'Anyway, he's twenty years older than her.'

'Is he? You old people all look the same to me.' I switched on the oven. 'But in general, if there was say, a really sweet, lovely, generous girl. Just a hypothetical girl. Not me.'

'Clearly not you from that description.'

'And let's say Hypothetical Hannah liked this

boy, but he already had a girlfriend, do you think it's possible for her to still be friends with the boy?'

Dad opened a bag of frozen chips. 'That depends, is this Hannah going to cry with envy every time she sees the boy? Or the girlfriend?'

'No! That is, I don't think Hannah is the weeping kind. More the punching kind. You know, in a sweet and generous way.'

Dad shook the chips onto a baking tray. 'That sounds about right, now that I recall your, ahem, I mean, most young people today's largely violent and vengeful nature.' He slid the chips into the oven. 'It's probably best to steer clear of any situation that's going to result in a punch-up.'

'But what if Hannah thought she could control her walloping urges, even though the girlfriend's attractive smiley face was begging for it?'

'Then I guess I'd ask, is this girl going to flirt with the boy?'

'Well, obviously she wouldn't flirt. That would be very rude.'

This didn't seem to make things any clearer for him.

'And I'm not rude, you banana! I mean, *Hannah's* not rude. She's a model of politeness. Like me.'

Dad spluttered.

'Well, I am when I'm outside this house,' I sighed. I have to admit that occasionally I am a bit short with my family. 'Sometimes I think there are evil forces in our home that drive me to door slamming and insults, and then I realise that it's you lot.'

Dad was slicing cucumber. 'Yes, well, thanks for the chat Faith, uplifting as ever. Overall, I would say that Hannah, and you, should be friends with whoever is prepared to put up with you. One day we'll be legally allowed to kick you out and you should probably line up a few floors to sleep on before then.'

'Thanks; you've been very helpful. I'd love to return the favour, so if you ever want someone to even out your bald spot, so that it doesn't look so much like the silhouette of a screaming monkey, I'd be more than happy to oblige.' Which was a nice parting shot because it meant I had the pleasure of watching Dad surreptitiously attempt to look at the back of his own head in the mirror for the rest of the day.

SUNDAY 29TH APRIL

When I came into the kitchen this morning I found Granny had popped over and that she was locked in some sort of combat with Sam. Her hands were around his throat so I assumed she was strangling him and started to back out the door.

'Don't mind me,' I said. 'I didn't see a thing.'

'Faith!' Granny called.

'Don't worry, you're busy. I'll come back later.'

'I need your help, Faith.'

'Sorry, Granny, I think it's better that you do Sam in on your own. After all, it won't matter much if you spend the rest of your days in prison because you haven't got many left, whereas I've got my whole life ahead of me.'

'Faith, get in here.'

So I opened the door. She was trying to put Sam in a bow tie.

'Oh, this is even better!' I said. 'Please tell me you're going to get a photo of this.'

Granny ignored me. 'Do you think he looks smart?'

'I think he looks like an idiot, which is much more enjoyable. For me.'

'Can't I just wear my jeans?' Sam asked. Along with his bow tie he was wearing the suit Mum bought him for Aunt Joyce's wedding two years ago. It showed off his ankles nicely.

'No,' Granny snapped. 'Mrs Moore's grandson never wears jeans.'

Sam pulled at his shirt collar. 'I don't want to go any more.'

'Of course you do. You like taking care of your elders, don't you?'

'Wait a minute,' I said. 'Do you mean you've got Sam waiting on you and your friends?' I turned on

Sam. 'How come you've never done that for your loving sister?'

'You never said you'd pay me.'

Granny frowned. 'Don't tell Mrs Moore that, I'll never hear the end of it. Try to look like you're doing it because you enjoy serving the community.'

'Let me get this straight,' I said, unwrapping a Twix that I'd just found in Granny's handbag. 'You're trying to use Sam to make you look good.'

'Well, obviously not Sam just as he comes,' Granny said. 'An improved version.'

'I'm standing right here!' Sam protested.

'I'm not sure that sticking a bowtie on him is going to turn him into an asset. It's a bit like putting a wig on a pig.'

Granny went at Sam with a comb. 'He's only got to hand round plates. Obviously, I'm not going to let him speak.'

'Obviously. Are sure about the plates? Have you considered just letting him hold one big silver platter like those butlers made out of wood? He could do that convincingly. In fact, you could forget about Sam and just go with the wooden butler.'

'Still here,' Sam said.

I licked my chocolatey fingers. 'Who are you trying to impress anyway?'

'I just want people on my over-fifties committee

to know that Mrs Moore isn't the only one with grandchildren. She thinks she's so wonderful; pretending her teeth are still her own and always parading her grandson about as if she's personally responsible for his grade eight in piano –' She swung round to look at Sam. 'You can't play the piano can you?'

'I can do "Kumbaya" on the tambourine.'

Granny turned back to me. 'He'll have to do.'

'What's your committee doing today?' I asked. 'You're not putting on a show again, are you? I haven't recovered from you doing the cancan yet.'

'I did give a powerful performance, didn't I? But we're not planning the show today; we're discussing our carnival float.'

Now, you'd think that making a carnival float would be a nice safe activity for the elderly, but my granny manages to make a spectacle of herself whatever the occasion. Last year, her over fifties-group's float had a caveman theme and Granny wore a furry mini-skirt and a bone in her hair.

'Would you like some suggestions for your float?' I asked. 'How about a Victorian theme? The Victorian liked nice long skirts, didn't they?'

'I think we'll go for something a bit more jazzy.'

'How about space and astronauts?' Sam suggested.

'That's a great idea,' I said. If Granny's head was

inside an astronaut's helmet no one would even know it was her. But she didn't seem keen.

I fished about for some more chocolate in Granny's bag but there wasn't any so I had a look through her makeup instead.

Granny sent Sam to polish his shoes then looked me up and down.

'I don't suppose you'd ever consider helping your old grandmother out?' she said in a low voice.

I've got to admit that I had been wondering why she was bothering wheeling Sam out when clearly I'm a much more impressive specimen.

'Does this mean that you recognise what a charming, intelligent credit to the family I am?'

She took back her lipstick in an unnecessarily grabby way. I hadn't even finished putting it on.

'It means that I know what a good liar you are,' she said.

'Thanks. It's genetic.'

'Does that mean you'll consider helping me?'

I pocketed her blusher. 'I'll email you a list of my prices.'

LATER

Ang rang me to say that her mum has agreed she can go on the French trip. 'I made a list of the all the ways I would benefit from the trip,' she said. 'And I added a list of things I could do around the house to earn it.'

'That's great.'

'Have you asked your parents?'

'Yep. Yesterday at tea I said, "Mum, Dad, third person I'm forced to share a house and a blood type with, whose name escapes me, I'm going to France."'

'Oh. What did they say?'

'Well, there was the usual irritating request for details, but in the end we all agreed that I have earned a break.'

Actually, Dad pointed out that the trip overlaps with Granny's stay so it might help make the house less crowded. He also said that it would be nice to have a bit of peace and quiet without me asking him for money. And he probably won't miss me pointing out that if he doesn't want vomiting at the breakfast table he really ought to keep his ear hair under control. Basically, as I've been saying for some time now, it's in everybody's interest for me to have a relaxing holiday.

LATER STILL

Sam's back. He says Granny's friends thought he was great. I'm not sure I believe him.

But then, old people do get excited about beige trousers, coach trips to Bognor, and all you-can-eat carvery so clearly they don't expect much from life.

And if you think about it, Sam's got a lot in common with a beige pair of trousers.

MONDAY 30TH APRIL

Icky heard me talking to Megs about the French exchange this morning.

'Oh God,' she interrupted. 'If I'd known you were coming I wouldn't have signed up. They're not seriously letting you go, are they?'

I gave her my haughtiest look. 'Well, obviously the school are very protective of me because I'm their star pupil, but since I've promised I'll come back they've agreed I can go. Although between me and you I'm pretty sure they're sending an undercover bodyguard to keep an eye on me.'

Icky snorted, snottily. 'You're delusional. They're probably hoping you'll fall in the Channel and sink like the fat lump you are.'

That's what I love about Icky. You expect her to be utterly evil and she always delivers. 'It's been delightful as ever, Vicky, we really must chit chat more often. Oh no, wait, actually, it's been truly revolting listening to your disappointment in yourself once again emerge as nonsensical vicious ramblings and I'd rather scoop my own eyes out with a chopstick than ever speak to you again. Yeah, that was it. Must dash.'

She got quite sweary and aggressive at that point, which was a mistake because Miss Ramsbottom has got a rude word radar and she swept down and started lecturing Icky. I managed to get in a smug look before we sauntered off to Chemistry.

'See?' I said to Megs. 'Icky is going on the trip. I need you there to protect me.'

'You're quite capable of doing your own walloping. Besides, it's a rip off; all that money and when you get there you still have to go to school.'

'You can't put a price on education, Megs. Or French pastries.'

But she still wouldn't agree. Lily hasn't changed her mind either, so at lunchtime, Angharad and I had another go at persuading them.

'Are you sure you don't want to come?' Ang asked Lily.

'The thing about France,' Lily said. 'Is that everything is in French, isn't it?'

'Yes,' Megs said.

Lily wrinkled her nose. 'I don't think I can be French.'

'Don't worry, I don't think the French want you,' I said.

'You don't have to speak French all the time,' Angharad said patting Lily's arm. 'The French are very good at speaking English.'

'Exactly,' I agreed. 'And if you get stuck there's always the international language of pointing. Or dancing. Remember in Year Eight when we did that dance about saving the rainforest and Mrs Williams said that you communicated powerfully through your movements?' (Actually what Lily's jerking and kicking communicated to me was that she was choking, but I didn't mention this.)

Lily stood up and shrugged. 'I still think I'll give it a miss. I'm a bit busy at the moment. I'm working on hatching something out.' She ambled off to get second helpings of pudding and we were left staring at each other.

'Hatching something?' Angharad repeated.

I held up my crossed fingers. 'Let's just hope it's a baby chick rather than an alien offspring.'

MAY

TUESDAY 1ST MAY

More school. It never stops. At lunchtime I said to the girls, 'Apparently these are supposed to be the best days of our lives.'

'What? Tuesdays?' Lily asked

'No, school days. We're supposed to be all young and carefree and skipping about singing. And we could be if it weren't for Miss Ramsbottom talking about mocks, and regulation hairdos and the futility of human existence all the time.'

'Because I prefer Wednesdays,' Lily said.

I sighed. 'I think that adults pretend this is a great time just to keep us here. They're afraid of us growing up and leaving home and eating ice cream for tea. It's all a lie.'

'Thursdays are probably the worst.'

'Anyway, it would be pretty miserable to think that Mr Hampton's lecture on the best way to clean a test tube was the peak of your life's happiness. I think the best days of my life will be when I make some kind of scientific breakthrough. ... On a tropical island ... While wearing diamonds.'

Lily nodded. 'Yeah, and that will probably be a Saturday, won't it? Most good stuff happens on a Saturday, so that's the best days of your life isn't it? Definitely Saturdays.'

'Exactly, because there's no school,' I said.

Megs looked from me to Lily and back again. 'If

Lily changes her mind and decides to go to France, promise me the two of you won't go anywhere alone together.'

'Are you getting jealous again?' I asked.

'No, I'm worrying that one of you will say, "Look out for that French lorry!" And the other one will say "Yes, I like baguette sandwiches too" and then get run over.'

I raised my eyebrows at Lily. Megs talks a lot of nonsense sometimes.

LATER

Anyway, what is Megs blithering on about? If I need protecting from an out of control French lorry, she'll be there to throw herself in front of it like a good friend.

WEDNESDAY 2ND MAY

After debating club we went to Juicy Lucy's. I wanted to prove to myself that I can get along with Ethan without getting all droopy about it, so I sat next to him. Obviously, that's the only reason I sat next to him and nothing to do with his shiny dark curls looking particularly lovely, or anything.

'Pretty good debate today,' I said. 'Something about Michael's speech reminded me of you. I think it was the part where he said, "It's obvious I'm right".'

He grinned. 'But when I say it, it's cute, yeah?'

'Oh, totally. Arrogant and conceited and cute.'

'Stop, you're overwhelming me with compliments.'

We chatted away about what Miss Ramsbottom's powers would be if she was a super villain. I said I'm pretty sure that Miss R has already got spidey sense because the minute I started thinking about painting Lily's shoes purple today, she appeared in the doorway of the art room and gave me a very stern look. Ethan pointed out that the chances of catching me planning mischief at any given time are quite high. It was a pretty good chat until Westy came over and gave Ethan a dig in the ribs.

Ethan stood up. 'Er, excuse me Faith. I can see Vicky looking happy and well-adjusted over there, so I'd better go and do something about that.' And he wandered off to where Icky was sitting. I wanted to go and listen to him take the micky out of her but Westy was hovering expectantly, so I said, 'All right, Westy?'

He cleared his throat.

'I got you a coke,' he said, putting it down and sloshing most of it over the table.

I mopped it up with a napkin. 'Thanks, that's really nice of you. I'll buy you one next time.'

He nodded.

'Are you going to sit down?'

'Oh. Yes. Yep, I'm going to sit down now.'

So he did.

I couldn't help noticing that he was being a bit funny.

'Are you okay, Westy?'

'Fine. I mean, I probably shouldn't have had that third helping of chilli at lunch, but I thought, you know, that it was best to keep my strength up. But I'm really sweating now.' He loosened his already loose tie. 'Phew, are you hot? I don't mean *hot* hot. I mean, obviously you are *hot* hot, but honestly that's not all I notice about you because you're really smart too.'

I looked round for Megs, but everyone had mysteriously melted away from our table.

Westy took a gulp of air. 'Faith, can I tell you something?'

I looked up at his nervous face and suddenly I had a really bad idea about what the something might be.

'Please don't, Westy,' I said.

'I've sort of psyched myself up now. It's a bit like when I did that white water rafting, as soon as you've got your nerve, you've got to go.'

'Didn't you capsize that raft?'

'Yeah, but I'm surprisingly buoyant.' He frowned, 'This speech isn't exactly going as I planned it. I don't know how I've got on to my Venture Scouts rafting holiday. Unless you like Scouts? Because I did actually get quite a lot of badges. I even sewed them on myself. I did once sew my pants to my trousers but that's why you really should take stuff off before you sew it ...'

'Westy, shall we go and sit with Elliot and Angharad?'

I thought that if I could get him with some other people I might be able to avoid what was coming next.

'Can I just say this thing? It's taken me a long time already. It's taken all the time I've known you.'

I tried to speak but he carried on.

'Because the time I've known you has been really good. Really, really good. Because you're so ... good.'

I thought my heart was going to break. 'Thanks, I think you're good too, but West—'

'I like you more than good. You're definitely an excellent ...' he swallowed. 'Faith, would you ever think about going out with me?'

I honestly have never thought about going out with Westy. I had no idea what to say because I knew I couldn't give him the answer he wanted. I hesitated, but Westy must have been able to tell from my face because his whole body sagged.

I put a hand on his arm. 'Westy—'

'Nah, course you don't want to go out with me.

Only kidding!' He tried to give me a playful punch, but it threw me sideways and I banged my head against the wall.

I wanted to cry.

'I think you're brilliant, Westy. You're a great mate.'

'Yeah.' He was looking at the floor. 'Yeah, okay, Faith.' He stood up. 'I've just got to … I'll see you later.'

I felt terrible.

I still feel terrible.

THURSDAY 3RD MAY

Why don't I fancy Westy? He's got a nice face; he's sweet and funny. It would be so much simpler if I liked him instead of Ethan. The thing is that just looking at Ethan makes me feel swoony inside. Staring at Westy doesn't exactly have that effect on me. Oh no, am I one of those people that's only interested in looks? Wait a minute, I split up with Finn, who is probably one of the best looking boys on the planet, because we didn't have anything in common.

Have I got things in common with Westy? I mean, we always seem to have plenty to chat about. We both like watching people fall over and large amounts of cake, but he's definitely a much bigger fan of wrestling and rugby than I am. And I'm pretty sure that I like reading and getting really good marks in Chemistry more than he does. He's great as a friend, but there isn't really anything beyond that matey level, at least not for me.

What I like about Ethan is that he makes me feel ... understood. He gets my sense of humour. He appreciates how I am not exactly fond of doing tons of homework, but I do like being top of the class. He knows how I enjoy insulting my family and friends even though I sort of, you know, love them a bit really. I suppose he understands all this because that's the way he is.

Hmm. Does this mean I only like people who remind me of myself?

That's a bit vain.

Even for me.

I don't know, I just like the way Ethan and I interact; we connect. Also, I've spent quite a lot of double RE lessons thinking about snogging his face off. I think that's a definite sign that you're quite keen on someone.

I don't feel that way about Westy.

FRIDAY 4TH MAY

I've decided to become a prefect. It happened at lunchtime.

Angharad said, 'They've got prefect application forms in the office.'

I said, 'Mmm hmm, they've also got a form you can fill in if you enjoy telling people their skirts are too short, and you want to spend time helping Miss Ramsbottom make up more pointless rules. Oh no, wait, that's the same form.'

Angharad gave me a reproachful look. 'I think it would be amazing to be a prefect.'

'It would look good on university applications,' Megs said.

Lily nodded. 'And you get that cool badge.'

'Oh come on, prefects are not the coolest people, or the nicest. And some of their methods are questionable. What about that PTA barbeque they had last year? Corinne Taylor got those cheeky Year Sevens to behave by vomiting on them.'

'I'm not sure she planned that,' Lily said. 'I think it was more to do with the fact the prefects were running the ice-cream stall and she'd been helping herself to free samples.'

That got my attention. 'Free samples?'

'Yep. And that's just one of the advantages to being a prefect,' Megs said, 'You also get actual permission to go into town at lunchtime.'

Angharad's big hopeful eyes were fixed on me; this was clearly something she wanted us all to do together.

'And they've got their own common room. I heard there's a toaster in there,' said Lily.

That did it. Ice cream and toast are precisely what I'm looking for in a remunerative package. I gave a decisive nod. 'As you know I have always been a keen upholder of the school charter. Angharad! Fetch us some forms!'

That was pretty much the extent of my decision making, but the more I think about it the more sense it makes. After all, I have a lot to offer.

I pointed this out to the girls when Ang came rushing back with what looked like an unnecessary large amount of paperwork.

'What exactly have you got to offer?' Lily asked.

I waved my hands about to indicate piles and piles of good stuff. 'Loads. It's like when they employ ex-criminals to help catch burglars. I know every way to break the rules in this school; I could give the teachers invaluable advice.'

'Isn't that going to spoil other people's fun?' Megs asked.

'I didn't say I was actually going to give them the advice – but they don't need to know that until I'm elected by a landslide.'

Megs shook her head. 'Prefects don't get elected.'

'Don't they? What is this, some kind of totalitarian state?' I remembered where I was. 'Don't even bother to answer that.'

'You have to apply,' Angharad said. 'That's what

the form is for. Then you get invited for an interview. Imagine if they chose you to be head girl!'

This was all news to me.

Megs poked me. 'It amazes me how little you know about this school; you've been coming here for nearly four years.'

'Yeah, but it's a bit like when you have to use those stinky loos in car parks; you just keep your eyes straight ahead and try not to let any of the filth rub off on you.'

They looked at me blankly. Even more blankly than usual.

'Or when you're forced to go to a DIY shop with your parents. You keep your eyes straight ahead and try to let as little boringness rub off on you as possible by humming something cheerful.'

Megs's eyebrows had knitted in an unattractive fashion. 'Do you honestly hum for entire school days?

I shrugged.

'Me too,' Lily said.

'Anyway,' said Megs. 'Back in the real world where there are rules and things. If you want to be a prefect you have to apply like Ang said. And if your application gets approved by your Head of Year then you have to do an interview with a selection committee.'

I groaned. 'I want to be a prefect, I don't want to adopt a baby.'

I leafed through one of the forms. It was three pages long.

'It would be easier to buy a gun,' I said.

'Prefects have more power than guns in this school,' Megs said.

It's certainly true that you wouldn't want Corrine Taylor firing all she's got at you.

SATURDAY 5TH MAY

We went bowling with the boys today. I was kind of apprehensive about seeing Westy because I still feel terrible about turning him down. But he never showed up.

When I arrived, Ethan was sat in the corner scowling into a coke. Even when he's grumpy he looks fit. His dark eyebrows were all scrunched and tortured and his eyes were burning into the table like he was thinking brilliantly funny, but wickedly biting, things to say about people. Obviously, I didn't exactly want to put myself in the firing line, but somehow I found myself drawn towards him. He looked up at me with his deep dark eyes and I couldn't stop myself from sitting down. For a second, I thought something fantastically witty was going to just trip off my tongue and then he'd laugh and we'd have a nice chat. What I actually said was, 'All right?'

Which wasn't quite as clever as I'd been hoping for.

Ethan just scowled some more.

Then I followed up on my stunning opening line by scratching my ear and saying, 'No Westy?'

Ethan twitched. 'I don't think he's coming. He's pretty cut up about you breaking his heart.'

It was like he'd punched me in the stomach.

'I didn't break his heart. I just said I thought it made more sense for us to be friends.'

His eyes flashed. 'I'm not sure you're in a great position to talk about sense. I don't think you've used a lot of sense choosing boyfriends, so far. And that's up to you, but maybe you shouldn't be messing with the emotions of decent people.'

I couldn't believe he was saying all this.

'Come on, Ethan. I really like Westy, but you can't honestly expect me to date someone who I'm completely unsuited to?'

'You didn't mind with Finn.'

That was harsh.

I took a deep breath. 'I'm sorry if he likes me. I didn't know.'

He gave me a long look. 'You know what Faith? For a smart girl it seems like there's a lot you don't notice.'

What the hell is that supposed to mean?

Then he said, 'I'm not in the mood for this, I'm going to go.'

And he did. Which seemed pretty rude to me.

I did a bit of bowling but I couldn't really concentrate on it. Megs pulled me into a seat next to her and Cam. 'You all right?' she asked. 'What did Ethan say to you?'

'He had a go at me for turning Westy down.'

'That's not very fair,' Megs said.

'Listen, Faith,' Cam said. 'Try not to take it personally, Ethan's been really moody today. I think he might be in trouble at home. When I got to his house this morning, I could hear his mum and dad shouting.'

'What were they saying?'

'I didn't listen, did I? I took a walk around the block and it was all quiet when I got back, but he's hardly said a word to me.'

Megs frowned. 'That's not an excuse for shouting at Faith just because she doesn't want to go out with Westy, is it?'

'No, I know. I'm just saying, he's not himself.'

It made me feel a tiny bit better but I keep thinking of Ethan looking at me like I'm some heartless cow.

Not a great day.

SUNDAY 6TH MAY

I rang Megs. 'I feel bad about Westy. Do you think I should have noticed? Do you think it's my fault?'

'It's no one's fault. You don't have to date

anyone you don't want to and no one should pressurise you.'

As you know I've always found Megs to be very sensible and generally right about stuff.

'Remember last year when I had that thing about Liam?' Megs asked.

Liam is Megs's cousin Andre's best friend. Two Christmases ago she was really into him.

'I remember.'

'And when Andre blabbed to Liam about me liking him I had to listen to the whole "I just don't like you in that way" thing.'

I had to listen to it too because it was all Megs talked about for a month.

'And it was really uncomfortable and horrible for a while, but after a bit I moved on and now I can have an entirely sane conversation with Liam. Things will go back to normal with Westy; you've just got to give it a bit of time.'

I hope she's right.

MONDAY 7TH MAY

We had a day off school today because it's a bank holiday. I don't know why anyone thinks that bank workers need a holiday. It can't be very stressful hanging out with large piles of cash every day. You could make yourself a nest of fifty pound notes and have a little sleep. A really luxurious sleep. Bankers should try spending time with Miss Ramsbottom. Then they'd need a holiday. Anyway, contrary to what Granny is always saying, I'm not entirely ungrateful and it is nice to have the weekend extended a bit.

I went on a picnic with the girls. Just as I was attempting to demonstrate that it is possible to put half a quiche in your mouth and my defences were down, Angharad whipped out the prefect forms again.

Lily and Megs got busy with their pens. Once I'd swallowed my quiche I said, 'Surely we can just write our names? They can't have that many applicants, can they? It's just a bit of twirling about wearing a shiny badge, isn't it?'

'Is that all you think the prefects do?' Megs asked.

'Of course not. Obviously they also put a lot of time and effort into looking down their smug noses at people.'

Lily giggled.

'And they steal the best seats from Year Sevens. If there's any time left over, I think they might poke about in the lost property.'

'I like that part,' Angharad said. 'It's nice to think of returning something to its rightful owner.'

'Oh, I don't think they go that far, Ang.' I said. 'They don't do anything efficient like reuniting people with their lost property; I think they just move it about a bit. You know, from the lost prop cupboard to the hall, spread it out on the stage, then outside on tables, to give it a little holiday, then pack it back in boxes. It never gets any less. In fact, I think it reproduces. Those jumpers and cardis get snuggly in the cupboard and before you know it they've brought forth a family of odd socks.'

Megs took a feeble normal-sized bite of what was left of the quiche. 'So that's your take on being a prefect is it? That it's similar to a zoo keeper trying to get pandas to have babies, only you're responsible for the reproductive life of jumpers?'

'You're forgetting the free food,' Lily said.

'I never forget the free food,' I said, scooping up the last of the crisps. 'And while you lot have been blithering on, I have almost finished my form. You can copy it if you like. Make sure you spell "genius of gargantuan proportions" correctly.'

TUESDAY 8TH MAY

I handed in our prefect applications today. Icky saw me going into the office with our forms and actually waited for me to come back out just so she could have a go.

'You are joking, aren't you?' she sneered. 'They're never going to choose you as a prefect.'

I gave her the withering look that I normally

reserve for when Granny asks me to give her a back rub. 'And you think you'd be better, do you?'

'I'll be brilliant. Everybody says so.'

'I've told you before, Vicky: when you think you can hear people saying nice things about you, it's actually just the voices in your head.'

She screwed up her face. 'There's nothing wrong with my head, and if any of your lot make it on to the prefect team I will eat it.'

'I'm not sure your pin head will make much of a snack. It's hollow, isn't it?

She stuck her tongue out. Proving once and for all just how mature she is.

LATER

Obviously, I don't care what Icky thinks about my prefect application, but I hope that Miss Ramsbottom doesn't share her opinion. I need her to approve it. I know that she's always disliked me and has generally made my life hell, but I think that even she can't question the fact that I am really good at telling people what to do.

EVEN LATER

I sent Westy a video of a pug in a hat making a cake. Dogs in hats aren't my favourite and I'm pretty sceptical that he cracked the eggs himself, but Westy loves that stuff. He sent me back a smiley face. Hopefully that means he doesn't completely hate me. It just seems unfair; no one is telling Ethan off for not reciprocating my feelings. I mean, if Westy is a victim then so am I; I'm totally into Ethan and I would really like to go out with him, but that's not going to happen and I like to think that I've accepted that and behaved with grace and dignity. Okay, so there was a little bit of sobbing, but I stopped after I covered Megs's T-shirt in snot. And maybe there's a tiny amount of obsessively imagining what it would be like if Ethan came to his senses and we could spend happy weekends being hilarious and feeding each other M&M's.

Oh God. Is Westy imagining feeding me chocolate? I need a lie down.

LATER STILL

Now I can't even enjoy a humble family-sized bag of M&M's. There's no pleasure left in life for me.

WEDNESDAY 9TH MAY

Today in French, Madame Badeau told us who we have been matched up with for the French exchange. My partner is called Josette. Seems like a reasonable name. Pretty French, but she can't help that. Mad Bad gave us photocopies of their forms and it looks like they had to answer the same stupid questions that we did.

For 'Who do you live with?' Josette had written: *I live with my vampire mother and my werewolf father in a cave. My twin sister does not like this paranormal stuff so she lives in a house. She is the boring one.*

I'm not sure that their forms were inspected by someone with the same eagle eyes for cheekiness that Miss Ramsbottom has, but I do think that I might get along with Josette.

I told Megs about her at lunchtime, but she didn't seem very interested. 'Do you want me to ask Madame if they've got any French girls left over for you?' I asked.

'No! I'm not asking my parents for a ton of money, just so I can meet a French teenager,' she said, as if I'd just offered Icky's trainers on a plate instead of the opportunity to broaden her horizons and mingle with fit French boys. I don't know what's going on. Something is wrong. I know this because I am a super-sensitive type who can pick up on other people's emotions. I will use my great powers of empathy to gently encourage her to tell me the truth.

Either that or I will beat it out of her.

THURSDAY 10TH MAY

Miss Ramsbottom stopped me in the corridor. She's like one of those policemen that enjoy doing stop and searches on innocent people all day just because it makes them feel big.

Anyway, I had to swallow the chocolate rabbit I was eating whole, just so I didn't have to listen to a lecture on how we're not supposed to eat while walking between lessons. Then I adjusted my face to the quiet and humble one that Miss Ramsbottom prefers.

It looks nothing like me.

'Faith, Madame Badeau informs me that you will be participating in the French exchange this year.'

I nodded. Humbly.

'I'm sure I need not point out ...' And yet she went right ahead and pointed it out anyway. '... That while you are in France you will be an ambassador for this school. In fact, for this country, therefore I expect you to be on your very best behaviour.'

'Yes, Miss Ramsbottom. I'm really looking forward to the opportunity to speak French with, you know, French people ... in France. I think the whole thing will be very educational.'

'I'm glad to hear you're enthusiastic. Please bear in mind that I can't possibly approve the prefect application of any student who brings the school into disrepute.'

It was at this point that I realised that she was staring at my cheek. When she finally flounced off I had a look in my pocket mirror. A sizeable portion of chocolate bunny ear was stuck to my face.

I'm not sure I'm going to make it to the prefect selection committee stage.

FRIDAY 11TH MAY

I was all excited at lunchtime, I said, 'Good news, Megs! Amber Dalgleish got so annoyed with her brother playing thrash metal that she went mad and kicked his drum kit, but she sliced her leg up so badly that you could see the bone.'

Megs pulled her sarcastic face. 'Wow! Yes, that's great. Or at least I can see how it's great for music lovers, and medical types that like looking at naked bits of bone instead of having them tucked up nicely in flesh like they're supposed to be. Why is it good news for me?'

'Because she was going on the French exchange! There's a space! You can come!'

'*Nrmp*,' Megs mumbled.

'Don't you *nrmp* me, I've just been to all the effort of inflecting three exclamations in my last sentence. You owe me exclamations. A squee at the very least.'

'Faith, I've told you I don't want to go on the French trip.'

'Yes, you do.'

'No, I don't.'

'I'll be there. You like me.'

'*Nrmp*.'

'And there will be chocolate and cheese. You love

chocolate and cheese, although you did promise you wouldn't combine them again after that night we made the Nutella pizza … Anyway, lots of lovely things. No school! That's lovely.'

'There'll be French school.'

'Well, no one will expect you to understand that. Even French kids couldn't be expected to pay much attention there. That's why they're so famous for that shruggy shrug thing they do. The teacher says *Qu-est ce que le point de l'ecole?* And the kids all do the Gaelic shruggy shrug, *Je ne sais pas!* And the teacher pushes back her beret and says *ah oui! C'est vrai! Il n'y a pas de point de l'ecole, let's all go to the café and have croque monsieurs instead! On y va!* That sounds civilised, doesn't it? Come on! There will hot French boys who will fall for our glamorous Englishness.'

'I'm not interested in French boys. I've got a boyfriend, even if you like to pretend he doesn't exist, and I'm not just going to disappear off and leave him!'

And then she stomped off. Proper stomping. I haven't clomped along that noisily since the last time Miss Ramsbottom said she had a headache. What on earth is going on with her? She seems properly upset. Which isn't like Megs at all. Usually she just pretends to be upset and then when I'm leaning in to see if she's alright, she pulls my hair and punches me on the nose. I miss those happy days. I've got to find out what's bothering her.

SATURDAY 12TH MAY

I'm fed up. Megs is being stroppy. Westy barely responds even when I send him hilarious pictures of kittens pretending to be circus performers. And Ethan ... well, despite the fact he is the one perverting the course of true love by dating someone who isn't me, Ethan seems to be managing to be cross with me. Which is outrageous. And quite depressing. I was trying to deal with the fact that he doesn't want to go out with me and I don't think I can handle him hating me too.

LATER

Why would anyone hate me anyway? I'm very good natured and always kind to young children and the elderly. Maybe he's just lashing out because we can't be together. Except we could, if he'd just dump Dawn. It's really very simple. Maybe I should draw him a diagram.

SUNDAY 13TH MAY

Josette phoned me earlier. When I picked up the phone she said. 'Allo? Faith? It's meeeeee!'

I was a bit confused about who 'meeeeee' was; you'd think that the French accent might have given it away, but sometimes on the phone Megs likes to do voices. I enjoy her Swedish accent so much that I've told her that when we have to change our identities and go on the run (which Granny has said she is pretty sure is inevitable) she should go Swedish full time. Anyway, I like to keep my cool so I just said.

'Yes! It's yoooooooou!'

Then we both laughed.

'It is Josette. How are you Faith? I 'ope your mother is well.'

Which threw me a bit. I said, 'She's never entirely well. She says it's stress from work and nightmare children, but I think she might be drinking when no one's looking. To be fair, you can't expect complete mental stability from someone who lived with my granny for twenty years.'

'Mmm hmm,' said Josette. 'This is good.'

I wasn't sure how much she'd understood.

'And I think she may have passed on some craziness to my brother. He's really odd.'

'I do not have a brother, but my sister she is called Delphine.'

'Dolphin?'

'Delphine.'

I don't think that's much better, but I was being polite so instead I asked, 'Do you get on with her?'

'Get on?'

'Do you like her?'

'Ah yes, she is my twin, but she is a good girl. Me, I am not so good.'

'No, I'm not so good either.'

We laughed again.

'So I'm coming to visit you soon,' I said.

'Yes, soon. You come to my house and we will have good times.'

That sounded promising. 'Is there a lot to do where you live?'

'To do?'

'You know places to, er, *aller? Le cinema, la discoteque,* um, *la patisserie?*'

'Ah, no.'

'No?'

'No. My village is ... little. Very little.'

'So what do you do? Where do you go to have fun?'

'*Pas de panique!* I always have big fun. You will have fun also.'

To be honest while communication wasn't entirely clear, if the amount we laughed is any indication, I think that we really will have fun.

MONDAY 14TH MAY

I had one last attempt to get Megs to see sense. 'I really think this is your absolutely last chance to get in on the trip,' I said to her. 'We should find Madame

Badeau at lunchtime and see if they can still fit you in.'

'Faith, I'm not going. Now, just shut up about it.'

'What's the problem? You can tell me.' I put an arm around her.

She shrugged me off. 'I just don't want to go.'

'Why not? Don't you think it would be fun?'

'Maybe. But I can't just drop everything for a week.'

'What do you mean "everything"? You're a fifteen-year-old school girl not the prime minister. Is this about Cam? Is that the whole reason you're not coming on our trip of a lifetime? Because you can't leave Cameron for a week?'

'Just leave it, Faith!'

And then she completely ignored me for the rest of the lesson, which was particularly unkind because Mr Hampton was reading from the text book and I could have done with a little chit chat to drown him out.

TUESDAY 15TH MAY

Megs is still not coming on the French trip, but Icky definitely is. And not only is she going to be in the same country as me, she's going to be in the same house. It turns out that Josette's twin sister is also doing the exchange and she's been paired with Icky.

Since Megs has banned the 'F' word and I'm not allowed to talk about anything French with her, I found myself in the ridiculous situation of actually sharing my misery with my mother. She wasn't very helpful.

'You'll be fine,' she said without taking her eyes off her detective programme.

I huffed. 'Honestly, anyone would think you were more interested in finding out who killed the vicar than hearing the inner most thoughts of your only child.'

'You're not my only child.'

'You know what I mean, your most important child.'

'Hmm.' She peered around me to get a better look at the screen. 'Like I said, I think you'll be okay.'

'I'm not sure you appreciate the magnitude of the problem.'

'It's only for a week.'

'It's quite hard for me to cope with Icky being inside the same school as me. Even though it is quite a large school and we are rarely in the same classroom, the poisonous nature of Icky means that I have already had a fist fight with her this term.'

Mum finally took her eyes off the telly and glared at me.

Whoops. 'Well, less of an actual fight and more of a disagreement.'

'Faith, please tell me you haven't been in a punch up.'

'It doesn't count as punch up if no one draws blood, right? Or maybe there was a tiny bit of blood, but Icky was wearing our horrible maroon PE kit, so it wasn't like you could notice it much.'

Mum ran a hand through her hair. 'What on earth is going to happen when you're put in a house with this girl?'

'That's what I've been trying to tell you! Listen, I think that if I really focus on ignoring her then I can probably get through this.'

'Good.'

'You're going to need to buy me some pepper spray though.'

'Faith! Don't be ridiculous. Just because you don't like the poor girl, you can't attack her with pepper spray.'

'I'm not going to use it!' I shook my head at her complete lack of faith in me. 'I'm just going to threaten her with it. Actually, that terrible patchouli perfume you've got would probably have the same effect on someone's eyes.'

Mum took a long shuddery breath. 'If you still want to go to France, you're going to have to promise me that you won't spray anything in anyone's eyes.'

I spread my hands in a gesture of innocence. 'All right! I won't.'

And I totally intend to keep that promise.

Unless Icky is really annoying.

WEDNESDAY 16TH MAY

Since Angharad and I are going to be away for a whole nine days Lily arranged for us to go to Juicy Lucy's with the boys after debating club. I wasn't really looking forward to it since Megs, Ethan and Westy all seem to be mad at me.

On the way there Ethan said, 'Can I have a word?'

'Okay, as long as you're not going to try to guilt trip me into a relationship with someone I can't help not fancying.'

He looked a bit sheepish. 'Yeah, the word I'm looking for is that one that people say when they've screwed up. Obviously, I've never been wrong in my life before so I'm struggling to remember what it is. Starts with an 's'.'

'And ends with a "–orry I was a total idiot?"'

He gave me a nervous smile. 'That's it. I *am* sorry. It's none of my business and it's not your fault that Westy's a bit hung up on you.'

'I didn't want to upset him,' I said. 'But I don't think giving him false hope was the answer.'

'I know and you're right. You're completely right. I was just having a bad day and it made me sad that Westy was unhappy.'

'It makes me sad too. Is he all right?'

Just at that moment Westy charged past us with Cam on his back shouting, 'Dino power!' Westy gave a very convincing roar.

'I think he's getting there,' Ethan said.

I watched Westy leap over a rubbish bin. 'I don't want to lose him as a friend,' I said. 'Or you.'

Ethan turned to look right at me with his big dark eyes and my insides went a bit swooshy.

'Westy is still your friend,' he said. 'And so am I. And I am deeply sorry for being an idiot, and you are completely free to date or not date whoever you like – it's none of my business.'

Which wasn't the best thing he could say because I wish it was his business who I date (i.e. HIM!). But I managed to pull a face which I hope suggested that he was forgiven.

'Hey, have you and Megan fallen out?' he asked. 'You two were very quiet at debating; normally, you keep up a running commentary. I couldn't believe it when neither of you had anything to say when Ryan took off his jumper and flashed us his nips.'

I sighed. 'Maybe we just weren't in the mood.'

Then to really cheer me up I spotted Dawn waiting outside Juicy Lucy's.

Ethan's face broke into a grin and he went up and stood really close to her. Imagine what it would be like to be that near to Ethan. With his lovely pouty mouth just centimetres from yours.

'You,' he said to Dawn, 'are exactly the person I wanted to see.'

'And that,' she gave him a sultry look, 'is exactly what I wanted to hear.'

And then she grabbed his arm and pulled him into Juicy Lucy's.

So that was nice. For them. For me it was mostly a bit of sick in the back of the mouth, followed by an aching loneliness inside.

At least Ethan is my friend again.

Inside, I chatted to Ang and Elliot. It's a good job they can still bear to have a conversation with me because I had the distinct impression that both Megs and Westy were keeping their distance. When it was time to go I managed to corner one of them, at least.

'So I'm off to France this weekend,' I said to Westy.

He looked at my knees. 'Yeah, that should be good. We went on holiday there once. They've got these really good cakes. You've got to watch it though, because when you point at stuff in the shop, they're not that great at understanding, and you might end up with the whole cake. I mean, that wasn't a problem because, actually, all that cream just slips down, but those posh bakeries are quite pricey.'

I laughed. 'I'll be careful. Although I am definitely planning on eating a lot of cake.'

Westy managed to raise his eyes to my left shoulder. 'You probably won't have any problems communicating though; I bet you're really good at French. You're way smarter than me, that's probably why ...'

'Oh, come on, Westy! That's rubbish. You're smart. You're the only person I know that's used trigonometry to calculate the best launch angles for water bombs. And you're the first person I would ask if I needed help with my computer. And you're not just smart, you're sweet and funny too.'

Westy was bright red by this point.

I scrunched down so he was at least sort of looking at me. 'I think you'd make a great boyfriend. I just ...' I lowered my voice. 'I kind of like someone who doesn't like me back and I have done for a long time, so I'm not really looking for a relationship.'

His eyes widened. 'Oh. I didn't know.' He jammed his hands in his pockets. 'Sucks, doesn't it?'

I nodded.

He jiggled about a bit. 'Listen Faith, can we just, you know, be like how we were before?'

'I would really really like that.'

He managed a half smile. 'I hope you have a good time in France.'

I still feel sad about the whole thing, but I

think that Megs is right: it will get back to normal eventually. I tried to tell her this, which you would have thought she would enjoy because being right is one of her favourite things, but, shockingly, Meg isn't as easy to corner as Westy and she's still being frosty with me.

THURSDAY 17TH MAY

During registration Mrs Webber was flipping through exercise books and scribbling things down in an even more furtive fashion than usual. I think her gambling habit interferes with her weekend marking time.

I watched her for a minute. 'Why do you keep switching pens?' I asked.

'You know me, Faith,' she said without taking her eyes off the book. 'I like to make the world a more colourful place.'

It's certainly true that she's got an inability to wear matching socks. But I had a strong suspicion that she was attempting to make it look like the books had been marked at different times over the last few weeks.

'Your dedication to our education is an inspiration to us all, Mrs Webber.'

She looked up. 'That reminds me: Miss Ramsbottom tells me you're looking forward to improving your French next week.'

I smirked.

'Which is funny because I was fairly certain that I heard you tell Lily that what you were most looking forward to was "Hot French Boys and eating your weight in pain au chocolat".'

'You didn't tell Miss Ramsbottom that, did you?'

'Of course not. Neither of us want you stuck here next week, do we? Anyway, she did tell me to let you know that due to your impressive levels of enthusiasm she wants you to be the person to give a report on the French trip in the celebration assembly the week after half term.'

I rolled my eyes. Typical Ramsbottom, always trying to take something fun and insert a bit of deathly dull into it.

'So you should probably make a few notes while you're there and perhaps try not to burn anything down.'

'It's certainly a nice suggestion, Mrs W, I'll bear it in mind.'

But she'd gone back to her forgery.

FRIDAY 18TH MAY

I ought to be skipping about making sure I've packed enough bracelets and nail varnish, instead I'm feeling rubbish.

It's as if someone is taking the mickey out of my plans to be a super good friend. My bestie isn't talking to me and I don't know how I'm supposed to make new friends in France when I've got to live with my worst enemy for a week.

If it was happening to someone else it might be funny.

LATER

Although, when you think about it, it is happening to someone else; it's happening to Icky. She must be really annoyed that she's got to share a house with me.

That idea has cheered me up a bit.

It's like Granny says, it's an ill wind that doesn't blow some idiot away.

LATERER

Just got a text from Megs. It says, 'Have a good time you big pig.' I welled up when I read it. That girl has got a wonderful way with words. It's a talent I share so I sent one back saying 'Thanks you toad.'

I hope this means she loves me again.

SATURDAY 19TH MAY

This morning Dad drove me to school. I expected to see Miss Ramsbottom skulking back from a night's hunting, but it was just the French teachers flapping about. Madame Badeau was looking particularly stressed for someone about to go on holiday.

I said to Dad, 'Thanks for the lift. I'm off to embark on my jet-set lifestyle. From Paris I might just head straight to Madrid. Then I'll probably be invited to the Cannes film festival. If I get spotted by a Hollywood producer I'll send you a postcard before I set off for the States, but whatever happens, don't let Mum turn my bedroom into a permanent granny flat.'

Dad nodded slowly. 'Yes, of course.' He put a hand on my shoulder. 'Right, now we've covered what's happening in your imagination, let's have a quick think about what might be happening in the real world.'

I pulled a face.

'I'll keep it brief. First of all, be really polite with your host family. You know how you are with me and Mum? Just do the exact opposite.'

'Seriously, Dad, obviously I don't treat other people like I treat you! Not unless I really don't like them.'

'I see.'

'What else did you want to say?'

He took a deep breath. 'No fighting, no fires, no disappearing, no driving, no smoking, no drinking, no imprisoning anyone even if they have stolen your pencil case—'

'Dad! That was years ago.'

'No explosions, no knives, no digging holes

unless that's exactly what you've been asked to do, no swimming anywhere with a big sign that says "no swimming", no extreme sports, no eloping, no joining a religious cult, and absolutely no sparking any kind of diplomatic incident. I don't want to be conscripted into the army to fight a war that you've started.'

He was panting a bit. He really ought to think about doing some cardio.

'Is that it?' I asked. 'Because you honestly don't need to worry, I was only really thinking about doing one of those things. Three or four at the most.'

He crossed his eyes. 'Every time you think of doing anything just picture my face.'

'I can't think of your face the whole time! How will I keep my food down?' Then I took pity on him and gave him a squeeze. 'Don't worry about me, you fried egg! I promise to keep the delicate balance of having a good time and not incurring any expensive damages for you to pay for.'

'I suppose that will have to do.'

I got my cases out of the boot and signed in with Madame Badeau.

When it was time to go Dad said, 'One more thing, Faith.'

'Yes?'

'Have fun.'

I let him kiss me on the cheek.

LATER

Finally, we were on our way. The journey was pretty dull. I think I'll recommend to Miss Ramsbottom that future school trips use more high-end transport like jets and limousines. I passed a bit of time by imagining what Josette's chateau would look like. I was thinking something *Beauty and the Beast*-ish. Preferably including the talking clock butler and the dancing crockery.

After that I tried to calm Angharad's nerves by listening to her fears whilst eating all her sweets. Poor old Ang really is quite fretty about the whole thing.

She bit her lip. 'Maybe I shouldn't have come. I'm missing a maths tutoring session and now my Year Sevens will fall behind.'

'No they won't. You've taught them so well they could probably do their GCSE now.'

'What if Louise doesn't like me?'

'Everybody likes you. A million people told you to have a nice trip yesterday. I didn't even recognise some of them. You're the most likeable person I know.'

'What if Louise's parents don't like me?'

I wasn't having that. 'Ang, you're clean and polite and you enjoy doing homework. Parents adore you. You'd better be careful they don't try and swap you for their own rubbishy French offspring.' She managed to smile at that, but I'm going to have to keep an eye on her. When I'm sad I always manage to reach out and let people know. Usually, by sobbing nosily or expressing my feelings by painting them on walls, but Ang tends to keep it quiet. I could tell she was still bothered because there was a big crease between her eyebrows and she was staring off into space. She's scared of meeting new people.

I rummaged around in my bag and pulled out Scruffy the dog, my exam mascot.

'Here,' I said, handing him to Ang. 'I want you to look after him.'

Angharad gasped like I'd just handed her a diamond necklace (which, by the way, is what I had actually asked for when my Mum said that she'd buy me something to take into exams with me).

'I can't take Scruffy! He's your good luck charm.'

'I want you to. This way if you get really miserable and it's too late at night to text me then you can give Scruffy a squeeze and remember that it's only for nine days and I'll be waiting to cheer you up in the morning.'

'Thanks Faith, that's real—'

'That's alright. Now, you don't mind if I have this last packet of wine gums, do you?'

I settled back to enjoy some scenery, but roads are pretty dull wherever you're looking at them. Ang had brought a few books to read so I flicked open a Tintin but it was all in French.

'I've picked up loads of vocabulary from that one,' she said. '*Saperlipopette!*'

'Bless you.'

'No, it's French. *Saperlipopette.*'

'What does it mean?'

'You say it when you're surprised. It's like goodness gracious! or something like that.'

Personally, I think being able to say '*Trois tranches de gateau, s'il vous plait*' is going to be far more helpful than '*saperlipopette*', but it seemed to be calming to Ang to tell me words that French grannies might find useful so I let her witter on.

We eventually arrived at Josette's school. It looks a lot like our school (i.e. large and horrible and easily confused with a prison). As soon as I got off the coach I was almost knocked flying by a bellowing girl.

'It is you!' And she threw an arm around me and started dragging me sideways.

'Josette?'

'Yes, and you are Faith.'

'I know. It's really nice to meet you. Journey was a bit of a nightmare. It looks like a little skip on the map, doesn't it?'

Josette nodded enthusiastically and then burst into peels of laugh. I wasn't sure if she hadn't understood what I said or if she was just bubbling over with the joy of meeting me. Which is understandable.

'I like your boots,' I said.

She was wearing some hefty looking lace up clompers like the kind of thing that builders wear to protect their toes from falling bits of house.

'Ah, these boots they are good for the kicking and the ...' she mimed grinding something underfoot.

'Squishing?'

'Yes.'

'So we're going to your house next? Listen, there's something I've got to tell you about Delphine's partner.'

'Delphine?' She looked over at a girl with the same shiny black hair she had, talking to Icky.

'Yes, her English girl. She's not my friend. She's my enemy. And she's not nice. *Pas de tout.*'

'Josette's eyes widened. 'Ohhh, this girl, she is bad?'

'Really bad. Rude, mean, wears perfume that smells like one of those freshener things that hang over the edge of the loo seat.'

'Delphine will not let her be bad.'

'Really?'

'Delphine she is my twin. She knows what to do with the bad girls.'

Before we went off in Josette's mum's car I

decided it would be a good idea to have a little word with Angharad's exchange girl. When I located Ang she was standing shyly with a beautiful French girl with bouncing chestnut hair.

'Ang,' I said, 'this is Josette.' Then I left Josette to babble on to her while I drew Lovely Locks to one side.

'Hi,' I said. 'I'm Faith, Angharad's friend.'

''Allo, my name is Louise.'

'So the thing is Lou, I need you to take extra good care of Angharad. She's very smart and cool, but she does worry about things and she was really nervous about this trip so I just need to know that you're going to look after her.'

Louise seemed confused.

'I will 'elp her with her French, yes?'

'To be honest, that's not really what she needs the help with. She's super-deluxe at French. In fact she's an intellectual giant, it's just that she's got the voice of a mouse. A lovely mouse. A kind, cheerful, generous cheese-sharing sort of a mouse, but one that everyone should be very kind to. Otherwise, her big ratty mate will duff them up.'

Even though I think in future I will avoid comparing myself to a rat, I felt that I'd made my point.

Louise seemed less clear. 'What is this mouse?' she asked.

'Just be kind to Angharad. Please.'

'Of course. I like Angharad. Of course I will be kind.'

And she turned away.

She'd better keep her word or I might upgrade myself from a rat to one of those bitey little dogs.

LATER STILL

I'm very tired. It's hard work not understanding a word people are saying. I wonder how Angharad is doing. She'll be missing her mum. I might just send her a supportive little text.

Josette seems really nice. She doesn't live in a chateau, just a middle-sized house, but fortunately she does at least have her own bedroom, which may help cut down the chances of Icky strangling me in my sleep. Or vice versa.

SUNDAY 20TH MAY

Today we went on a hike. Josette said we were going up a hill. That was the word she used. It was not a hill. It was definitely a mountain. The problem is that I can't really blame her for inaccurate language because I am having similar problems communicating in French.

This morning I thought that Mrs Josette was looking particularly fetching with her hair in a chignon (which is exactly the kind of tidy hairstyle

I'm always suggesting to my mum but she prefers to let her hair run wild and free and end up in the butter). Anyway, just to prove Icky wrong when she said that I don't know any French, I thought I'd try a little conversation, so I said to Mrs Josette, '*J'aime votre cheval.*'

Mrs J's eyes widened. She looked over her shoulder and then she started firing questions at Josette.

It turns out that I had complimented her horse (*cheval*) instead of her hair (*cheveux*). Josette also explained that she did once try to keep a baby goat in her room without telling her mum so I could see why my remark might make her nervous. In fact we had to spend the rest of breakfast reassuring her that there absolutely was not a horse in the house. Or a pig. Or a cow.

I hope we do animals in French when I get back to school because I've learnt some good ones.

Anyway, as soon as Josette and I had settled in our bus seats behind Angharad and Louise I leant round and whispered to Ang, 'How's it going?'

She smiled. 'Pretty good,' she whispered back. 'They're really nice. And they can understand me when I speak French!'

I beamed back at her. I knew she'd be fine.

When we arrived at the foot of the mountain Angharad looked even happier. 'Isn't it lovely?' she said. 'It's got a really French feel, hasn't it?'

I was pretty unimpressed with the view until a really fit boy with his hair in cornrows cheered up all the nature stuff by standing in my eye line.

'Who's that?' I asked Josette.

Rather than giving me the low down on Mr Fit in a nice discrete whisper Josette made a noise. A very loud French noise.

'*Eurrrp!*'she said.

The boy turned around.

Josette waved him over.

'Philippe, *mon amie*, Faith.'

Philippe gave me a long look. I looked him long right back.

His full-lipped French mouth broke into a wide grin.

'Are you walking?' he asked. 'Walk with me.'

I felt a little more enthusiastic about the whole walking business.

The teacher gave some sort of signal and we all set off in little groups. Josette walked with us, but occasionally stopped to point at things and exclaim loudly. While she was getting excited about a rock that looked like a dog, I snuck a look at Philippe. 'So . . .' I said. 'You're friends with Josette?'

'Ah, Josette. All the world, they know Josette.'

I wasn't surprised to hear this. People like Josette can't help being noticed. Well, they could help it if they didn't stand in the middle of a bus full of teenagers and shout 'Guess what I have in my socks?' but where would be the fun in that? (Obviously, I couldn't entirely understand what she had said about her socks at first, but I can tell you that all the pointing and foot waggling was pretty attention-grabbing even in French.) It reminded me of that time I lost my voice and Miss Ramsbottom accused me of smuggling jelly beans in my shoes and I had to defend my honour using the power of mime. Josette and I are actually a bit similar. I suppose that some people in life are wagglers and some are not.

At first, the mountain wasn't that annoying. The incline wasn't too bad; there was a clear path along the grass and Philippe was telling funny stories about all the crazy things Josette has done and I was telling him some stories about crazy things I've done (or sometimes, when the things were a bit embarrassing, I said that Megs had done them). After a while, I had to be a bit less colourful with the descriptions because I was starting to get out of breath. And then I had to focus hard on just walking.

Eventually, Philippe said, 'There is the top.'

When he said 'there' I assumed that he meant 'there' right in front of us. It turned out that he was pointing to a place still very far away. If I had known it was that far away at the beginning I would have cried.

I kept my head down and plodded on.

I walked and walked.

When I finally looked up the top had gotten further away. I'm not kidding you. After that I kept my eye on it. Even so, I started to feel like you do when you try and run up an escalator that's going down, I was practically jogging just to stand still.

I walked some more.

It became obvious that I was going to end my days trying to get to the top of this stupid mountain, so I said a silent prayer for my parents and Sam; I could only imagine how empty a life without me would be. I envisioned my own funeral and hoped that Megs would remember that I've said I don't want a fuss and that just the glass carriage with the horses wearing those black feathers, and the giant sculpture of me in flowers would be quite enough of a send-off, unless people really insisted on fireworks and closing all the schools. Then I started thinking about Megs and I wished she was here. And not just because I needed a piggy-back. Philippe interrupted my thoughts of Megs's dear old ugly mug to say, 'It is the top.'

And it was.

'It's nice, yes?' Philippe asked.

I didn't have enough breath to tell him that although it was lovely I was now pantingly aware that I could have bought a postcard and then enjoyed the view and adequate amounts of oxygen at the same time, so I just nodded.

While I was still puffing the teachers unpacked a picnic that someone somewhere had made. There was a lot of it, which is one of my favourite things in a picnic and a lot of the food was made with cheese or cream (but not both) which is the other thing I really value in picnic items. So overall it was quite good.

I was so exhausted that I ate my share lying down. Fortunately, Angharad volunteered to ferry more cakes to me as the need arose. I was glad to see that she was still looking cheerful. Louise gave me a bit of an odd look, but she seemed pally with Ang, so I didn't make any violent animal gestures in her direction.

'So you're having a good time, then?' I asked Ang.

'Well, at first I was so nervous that I could hardly speak. But Louise is lovely and her family are great. They're really helping with my pronunciation. Last night they put on a play for me!'

She seemed pleased about watching some mad Frenches act for her so I smiled creamily.

'I think my vocabulary has improved already. The French are brilliant aren't they?'

I looked across the grass at where Philippe was talking to his exchange partner, Ollie. 'Yep. Brilliant.'

My four helpings of cake had stopped me feeling

so dizzy and I was starting to think that if I could get hold of a note letting me off PE for the rest of my life, and a helper monkey to assist me with any heavy lifting, my lungs might one day recover.

Then the teacher said it was time to go back down the mountain.

Angharad and Louise bounded off immediately. I groaned. My legs had seized up and I wasn't sure if I could even stand up gracefully let alone saunter down a mountain in an attractive fashion. Josette had pulled a worm out of the ground and was now running after Delphine with it. Actually running; I didn't think I'd ever run again.

'We will go?' Philippe asked.

'I don't know,' I said. 'I might just stay here a little longer.' I tried to get to my feet. 'In fact, I might just not bother going back at all.'

Philippe's forehead wrinkled. 'You are going to stay here?'

I nodded my head.

''ow long for?'

'Well … this seems as good a place as any to settle down. Nice view.' I pointed at the stream. 'En-suite swimming facilities.'

He looked at me as if I'd suggested moving into the worm's hole, but living my life out on top of a mountain seemed preferable to attempting to bend my knees again.

"'Ere, let me help you.'

And he took hold of my hand. Strangely, after that I found myself much more able to get along.

Although I might need one of those mobility scooters to get through the rest of the week.

LATER

I'm pleased to say that so far Josette seems pleasingly mad and affectionate. I can't understand half of what she's saying but she has given me three hugs, one Chinese burn and a packet of chocolate drops. These seem like friendly actions. I've replied with several squeezes, one wallop and a Curly Wurly I found in Angharad's coat pocket.

International relations aren't nearly as difficult as people make out.

LATER STILL

Icky, on the other hand, does not improve when you move her to another country. In fact, I suspect that even if you whisked Icky away to a magical land of unicorns and rainbows, and a banquet cooked by the fairy folk, she would still scrunch up her weasely little face and say, 'I don't like looking at mythical creatures of great beauty and drinking dew from a crystal goblet. I want a Heat magazine and a Diet Coke.' Which is mostly what she's been saying every time Josette's parents feed us or suggest something for us to do. Except she only says it behind their backs. To their faces she's all smarm and smirk – she is such a fake.

MONDAY 21ST MAY

You would think that taking something horrible (school) and adding something incomprehensible (French) would result in a pretty awful day, but actually going to school with Josette wasn't that bad. The constant hum of people speaking rapid French really acts as a sort of anaesthetic.

It was pretty obvious by the bulging eyes and screechy voices that the teachers were saying the same sort of drivel that they do in English schools, but it's even easier to let it wash over you when you can't tell whether they're saying, 'You're an irresponsible idiot!' or, 'How many times have I told you not to poke people in the eye with that?'. I did actually pick up some useful French in the science lab this afternoon: Josette's Chemistry teacher taught me how to say, 'Stop! Stop! You'll burn the whole place down!' by patiently repeating it every time Josette and I got creative and tried a few experiments that weren't in the textbook. I don't know why they don't teach us French like that at home. You know, phrases that are relevant and can be used in everyday life.

I was pleased to discover that Philippe is in quite

a few of Josette's classes. He is very nice looking and from the way the teachers were practically doing twirls every time he answered a question he seems clever too.

I don't know why my dad always says it would be a bad idea for me to go to a school with boys; I found that it was perfectly possible to eye up Philippe, and ignore the teacher just as well as I do back home.

I hunted Angharad out at lunchtime. She seems to be having a great time. 'Last night, Louise and her brothers took it in turns to point to things in the room and I had to tell them the French word for them. They got faster and faster, till I could hardly get the words out and then I forgot the word for mantelpiece ...'

My brain nearly melted at this point at the thought that anyone anywhere ever *knew* the French word for mantelpiece.

'... so I said 'Saperlipopette!' and now Louise says it every time we see a mantelpiece. It's so funny!'

It was nice to see her happy. 'Josette and I did something similar,' I said. 'I pointed to things I wanted to eat and she told me if they were worth bothering with or not.'

'So you learnt some French vocabulary?'

'Not exactly. But I can make a vomiting sound in a French accent.'

Ang laughed. 'I'm super glad I came, aren't you? Tomorrow Louise's parents are taking us to a museum and they're going to let me buy the tickets! In French!'

Blimey. I'm pleased she's having a good time, but what with the ticket buying and the pointing, how will Ang ever go back to our humdrum existence after all this glamour?

LATER

The only problem with this little holiday is Icky. For starters, it is quite revolting watching her suck up to Josette's parents and then say rude things about them when they're out of the room.

Secondly, she has been showing me up at Josette's school because she has been speaking French more than me. This is because she has totally cheated and learnt a load of useful words and phrases. You'd think the teachers would appreciate my more inventive approach to communication, which involves a wide range of skills like drawing little pictures, miming and the occasional bit of expressive dance.

Thirdly, she takes any opportunity to whisper something nasty in my ear. Tonight at dinner she leant over and said, 'If you eat anymore pastry you'll need two coach seats on the way home.' No one could expect me to refrain from getting violent under this sort of duress. Surely even Miss Ramsbottom would understand if I gave her a quick karate chop to the neck, as long as I leave it out of my report.

LATER STILL

I should probably start making some notes for that stupid report. I brought a notebook along especially, but so far all I've managed is to make a list of cheeses that I want Mum to have imported when I get home.

TUESDAY 22ND MAY

Icky Blundell has stooped to new depths. I knew she was a snake but it seems that she's a double snake with slugs on top.

When Josette, Delphine, Icky and I got back from school today Mrs Josette greeted us at the door and asked, 'What is this?'

Only of course she said 'Theez' because she is French and therefore a bit dramatic. I thought she was going to produce a severed head the way her eyes were bulging. Half a finger at the least. But then she held up a packet of cigarettes. Megs says I am prone to thinking that everyone is always looking at me, but there was no mistaking the fact that the question was directed my way.

'They aren't mine!' I said.

Mrs J narrowed her eyes.

'I don't smoke.'

'They were in your bed.'

I wondered who on earth they did belong to and what the hell they would be doing in my bed. Then I caught sight of Icky's gleeful face and I knew exactly what had happened.

I gave Icky a very hard stare.

Delphine said something in French about how none of us smoked, but Mrs J shook Delphine's hand off her arm and said to me, 'This is very bad.'

I tried my hardest to look innocent. I mean, I *am* innocent, but I haven't had much practice at it so I'm not sure I did a very good job. 'I don't know who they belong to,' I insisted and then I trod on Icky's foot to find out if she's more honest with a broken toe.

She's not.

'I promise they're not mine,' I said.

Mrs J was still glaring at me. I thought she might send me home right there.

'They are mine,' Josette said.

I knew that wasn't true. I tried to give Icky a filthy look, but she had busied herself admiring her shirt buttons.

Mrs J switched her glaring on to Josette and told Delphine to take the rest of us to the park.

Delphine grabbed Icky and me by the hand. I

had the sense that she and Josette had seen their mum like this before. I tried to say, 'Josette doesn't smoke, they're not hers either.' But Delphine gave me a little shove down the drive.

We walked along the road in silence. When we got to the edge of some woods Delphine sat down on a log and gave a big sigh.

'Your mum's really cross,' Icky said.

I turned on her. 'She's cross because she thinks Josette is smoking and the reason she thinks that is because you're a complete cow and you hid those cigarettes in my bed because you wanted to get me into trouble because you're jealous of me.'

Delphine's eyes widened. 'It was you?' she asked Icky.

Icky smirked. 'I don't know what she's talking about.'

'That's just your problem isn't it? It's your complete lack of understanding of what an utter witch you are that makes you think it's okay to get other people into trouble. What's Josette ever done to you?'

Delphine looked between the two of us and I could see that she believed me. She's heard enough of Icky's nasty remarks over the last couple of days to know what she's like.

'My mother will be angry with Josette,' she said to Icky. 'Josette has trouble with my mother and now, again ... You must say to my mother you are putting the cigarettes in the bed of Faith.'

Icky shrugged. 'Why don't you tell her?'

Delphine shook her head in disgust.

At this point I had to intervene. 'Delphine won't tell her and neither will I, because we're not snitches, we wouldn't grass you up even though you tried to get me into trouble and you've definitely got Josette into trouble. We're not like you; our sense of decency hasn't shrivelled and decayed through lack of use.'

She at least had the good grace to look a tiny bit uncomfortable before she rolled her eyes and walked off.

Delphine and I spent about an hour in the wood. I filled in the time by telling her all of the worst things that Icky has ever done. Delphine was pleasingly shocked. 'She is not nice.'

I nodded.

'Not nice at all. I do not think I want to go to her house.'

'I'm not sure she's got a house. She probably sleeps under a rock. That's what toads do, isn't it?'

Eventually, Delphine thought her mum might have had enough time to calm down so we went back.

Mr J was preparing supper and Mrs J was nowhere to be seen. Josette was in her room looking a bit worn out.

'They weren't mine, honestly,' I said.

She grinned. 'I know. You 'ave been in my house all these days, but I have not seen you with the cigarette. Not one time. And I think you are a girl for trouble, but I'm thinking when you get trouble you do not tell lies.'

Which seemed a pretty fair assessment of my personality.

'You know it was Vicky, don't you?'

She smiled again. 'I did not think it was Delphine.'

'So why did you say they were yours?'

She shrugged. 'So you don't get trouble from my mother.'

'It sounded like she gave you a lot of trouble.'

'I am used to it. I don't want for her to say you are ... how do you say? That your bad will make me bad. Then she will say I cannot go to your house.'

'But she doesn't mind if you make me bad?'

'She says if I do that she will ...' she pulled a hooked finger across her throat.

'Your mum reminds me of my mum sometimes.'

Supper was a little bit quiet to begin with, but Delphine and I kept up a fairly cheerful conversation about whether French animals have a French accent. (They definitely do; I heard a hen yesterday that sounded just like Madame Badeau when I tell her that there may be a slight problem with my homework.) After a bit Josette and her mum joined in. Mr J never seems to have much to say, and Icky, for once, kept her trap shut.

Afterwards, I volunteered me and Icky for the washing up and as soon as the others had left the kitchen I turned on the taps and started on her.

'Putting those cigarettes in my bed was a new low, even for you, Icky. I suppose the only way you can get people to like you is to make everyone else look bad.'

She pushed past me to dump a pile of plates in the sink. 'You're so ugly you always look bad, you don't need my help.'

'Yet, still you're trying to get me into trouble with Josette's parents. Why do you dislike me so much?'

'I don't dislike you.' She turned her hard little eyes on me. 'I hate your guts.'

'I know that comprehension isn't your strong point, but I was actually looking for something I don't already know, like a real reason. Why do you hate me?'

'Because you're an idiot.'

I scrubbed a cup vigorously and slapped it down on the draining board. She makes me so angry. 'If you dislike stupidity it makes it all the more strange that you manage to love yourself so much. I suppose you couldn't find anyone else for the job.'

'I've got loads of friends and you know it.'

'Ha! See, some people say that you're a moron, but you've just proved what I've always said, which is that you're a moron with a vivid imagination.'

'You think you're so clever.'

'Don't take my word for it – we'll have the GCSE results to prove it next summer.'

'Sucking up to teachers doesn't make you a genius.'

'Which is a shame otherwise you'd be getting some "A" stars.'

'You do realise that people are laughing at you, don't you?'

I didn't say anything but my stomach tightened.

'You're always making such a fool out of yourself. Slobbering all over Finn, getting stood up by poodle–boy Ethan.'

I clenched my fists. 'That's not what happened!'

'You might as well face up to the truth: you're always throwing yourself at boys and trying to get everyone to look at you. It's pathetic.'

'Just shut up you pigging cow!' And then I poured a glassful of soapy water all over her. It wasn't very mature, but it felt really good. And then I fled before she had chance to retaliate. I sidestepped around Mr Josette in the hallway and ran up to Josette's room. I was shaking; Icky is just vile. What the hell does she mean, throwing myself at boys?

I lay on my bed for ten minutes taking deep

breaths and waiting for my heart to stop thundering. I really wished I could phone Megs. My eyes might have got a bit leaky at that point.

The door slammed open and Josette came barrelling in with a big grin on her face.

'It is all good. My father, he knows the truth.'

I wiped my face with my sleeve and sat up. 'He knows the cigarettes were Vicky's?'

'Yes.'

'How?'

'He is listening to you and Vicky talking and he hears it all.'

I couldn't believe it. 'But he never ... I thought he didn't speak English.'

'Ah, he is a quiet one. He doesn't speak so much, but always he listens.'

'So he knows that she did it?'

She nodded.

'What are they going to do to her?'

Josette shrugged. 'Nothing, she is not their daughter, but I say to you this: I do not think Vicky is their favourite girl and I do not think that Delphine will go to stay with her.'

'And you're not in trouble anymore?'

She grinned. 'Not this day.'

I was so pleased that me and Josette weren't in trouble. Although, I couldn't help wishing that Josette's parents had chosen to punish Icky. Maybe by sending her home and making her swim the channel to get there.

I gave Josette a hug. She squeezed me back.

'Faith, my father he knows the English, but he asked me to ask you to tell to him one thing.'

'What's that?'

'What is a pigging cow?'

WEDNESDAY 23RD MAY

This evening we are going to an 'entertainment'. The thing I've discovered about leisure activities planned by teachers is that you really shouldn't get your hopes up too high. A bit like life really. I'm just hoping that Philippe will be there.

LATER

Our entertainment was in the French equivalent of a village hall.

It was folk singing.

Seriously. When Josette's teachers sat down to plan how they were going to entertain a load of teenagers, I can't begin to imagine what made someone say, 'How about folk singing?' and I'm at even more of a loss to understand why the other people in the room didn't first, laugh at the ridiculousness of this suggestion, and then shoot the suggester just to make sure they never had to listen to any of their insane ideas again.

One of my Granny's boyfriends has a nasty habit of bursting into traditional Devonshire ballads when you're least expecting it. They're pretty bad. But at least they seem to have some sort of story to them, tonight I couldn't even understand what this lot were singing about. Which means I was just left with the melody, or lack thereof. Terrible.

I sat there with the old men warbling in one ear and Angharad in the other, explaining to me about how it was a cultural experience. She even tried to get me to help her look up words in a dictionary, until I reached my breaking point.

'When's this torture going to end?' I asked Angharad.

'Well, I think there'll be a bit more,' she said. 'They're only half way through the first song.'

It was like that stupid mountain all over again.

If Megs had been there, at least she would have told me a few beard jokes. When I'd taken as much as I could stand, I suggested that Josette and I treated ourselves with a trip to the loos.

The loos were not that treaty.

But on the plus side, when I flushed I could hardly hear the singing at all.

Back out in the corridor, we found Philippe and Ollie hanging about, looking tall and attractive.

'Hello, Faith,' Philippe said.

I didn't have a smart reply for that so I went with, 'Hi.'

'It is not so good, hey?' He nodded towards the singers.

'It's terrible,' I agreed.

'You want to go? Now? With me and Ollie?'

I wasn't sure there was anywhere else to go, but the not-being-in-the-same-place-as-the-singers part really appealed to me. I looked at Josette. She nodded. A lot.

I wondered if I should try to slip in and extricate Angharad, but when I peered back into the hall I could see her head bobbing about enthusiastically. She seemed happy where she was.

'There are teachers on the door,' Ollie said.

I could hear voices coming from outside the entrance door, which was ajar. It seemed unfair that the teachers got to skulk about in the cool night air. Were they there to keep us in or where they just distancing themselves from the 'music'?

'We can go like this ...' Philippe pointed to the stairs at the end of the corridor.

We went down the stairs and into some sort of storage space that was full of stacks of chairs and dusty cardboard boxes. 'Here,' Philippe said and cracked open what I couldn't help noticing was a pretty titchy window.

Josette swung herself up and through, and Ollie

followed behind. Philippe looked at me and made a 'you first' gesture.

Well, it's not that I disapprove of using windows to escape a situation (or, you know, cat flaps or any decent sized hole) but I wasn't sure how to do it gracefully.

I climbed up on a chair and stuck my head through. The window came out just above ground level. I put my right foot on the wall inside and took hold of the hand Josette was offering me. I pushed myself upwards off the chair. At least, I went up until everything above my hips was out the window, and then I stopped.

I was stuck.

'What is it?' Philippe said. His voice was a bit muffled due to the window being stoppered up with my backside.

So there I was, trying to work out the French for, 'I'm afraid my womanly behind has become lodged in your unfeasibly small French window' but all that came out was, 'Saperlipopette!'

Angharad and Tintin would have been proud.

Finally, with some tugging from Josette and Ollie I managed to wiggle my way through. When Philippe climbed out, all I could think was that he had been treated to the sight of my waggling bottom for the last few minutes, but it didn't seem to stop him smiling at me.

Or maybe that's *why* he was smiling at me.

I think the main thing we can learn from this is that even being stuck in a window is better than folk singing. Someone ought to tell Granny's boyfriend this. I would, but whenever I see him I find myself robbed of speech, because the whole of my being is consumed by wondering how anyone could possibly have so little hair on their head but so much up their nose.

Anyway ... we crept over the grass and through a line of trees into a field, making sure to stay out of sight from the bunch of teachers on the door.

People say that teenagers aren't very good at using their imaginations anymore and that we stay inside playing computer games and posting stuff on social media, and that we never get any fresh air and have lost the art of real life conversation. But that's really not true; once you introduce the opposite sex, I think you'll find that any teenager is happy to sit in a field and have a chat.

I really enjoyed the art of conversation with Philippe. We had a long chat about the differences between France and England.

'But even with all that,' I said. 'We've still got stuff in common. French teachers like forcing teenagers to listen to nonsense just as much as English ones, don't they? At home they make us listen to the teachers' barber shop quartet sometimes. It's nearly as bad as this.' I nodded in the direction of the singing.

'Yes, it is bad. I am listening many times because one of these singers is the friend of my father.'

'Which one?'

'With the nose like this . . .' he mimed a hooked nose. 'And the beard.'

'Oh, you mean the lady in the front row.'

He laughed. 'You are a very funny girl.'

That pleased me.

In fact, everything about Philippe pleased me. He was smart and nice and funny and fit.

'Hey,' he said touching me on the arm. 'Do you want to see Josette when she was climbing up the school?'

Inside, I was bashing cymbals together because he'd just touched my arm, but outside I did a very cool nod.

He shifted closer to me, and pulled out his phone. He actually did have pictures of Josette scaling the side of their school.

'What did your teachers say?' I asked. I put my hand on his as if to steady the phone so I could take a closer look, but to be honest I think we were both perfectly aware that no phone steadying was required.

'Oh, they say lots of things. Lots of loud, angry

things. They say *Josette! Get down or you will be killed! Josette come down to us and then we will kill you!*'

I laughed.

He slipped an arm around me.

I turned to look at him and I knew neither of us was thinking about Josette anymore. Then I leaned towards him and he leaned towards me and I knew there was going to be kissing.

Every part of me was tingling and then my lips met his. Wow. I think it's amazing how alive a bit of lip pressing can make you feel.

The wonderful thing about kissing is that it works whatever language you speak. The United Nations should bear that in mind.

THURSDAY 24TH MAY

This morning Mrs Josette asked us how the entertainment was last night. I was about to remark on how it's interesting that hairy old men manage to inflict their singing on young people no matter where you go, but Icky piped up with, 'Faith ran off with some creepy French boy.'

Mrs Josette looked as if a stream of quite frowny questions were coming my way, but Josette stopped her before she could get started by launching into a long explanation. I couldn't follow exactly what she was saying. There was a lot of gesturing. I think she was pretending to be a donkey at one point. Anyway, whatever she said, in the end Mrs J gave me a smile and said, 'I am glad you are making friends.'

'Yes, I do enjoy being sociable,' I said. Icky mimed vomiting into her cereal.

I stuck a croissant in her ear.

Quite a productive morning really.

LATER

Icky came barging into the bathroom while I was cleaning my teeth before bed.

'When I'm head girl,' she said, as if anyone was listening to her. 'I'm going to ban you from all school trips.'

I said nothing.

Icky twitched. 'And I'll make sure you're always on litter pick-up duty.'

I calmly popped my toothbrush back in my sponge bag and sauntered towards the door looking straight through Icky as if she wasn't there. Just before I walked out, I sniffed the air, 'I must tell Josette's dad to take a look at the drains. There's suddenly a horrible smell in here.'

FRIDAY 25TH MAY

Tonight there was a disco at Josette's school. I don't know why anyone tries to hold a social event in a school. No one ever says, 'You know where would be nice for your birthday party? A prison.' Or, 'Why don't you have your wedding reception at the factory where you work your fingers to the bone, all day, every day?' So why do they think that teenagers want to have fun at the place where they are incarcerated and worked into the ground? It's pretty twisted.

I've heard old people criticising the young and saying we're pampered and don't know what hardship is – let me tell you, you've got to be pretty tough to manage to get snoggy in the spot where your coffee-breathed troll-teacher tore strips off you because you didn't know the difference between meiosis and mitosis.

Anyway, French kids are clearly as tough as English ones because there was a lot of snogging tonight.

I was looking forward to spending some more time with Philippe, but amazingly I actually felt quite relaxed about seeing him. I didn't even stress about what to wear. It's nice feeling so comfortable with someone, but a tiny little part of me did think about how dizzy I'd feel if I was going to a disco with Ethan.

I'd hardly had a chance to speak to Angharad since the folk singing so it was nice to catch up. She seems to be really popular with Louise and her friends.

'How's it going?' I asked her.

'Brilliant. I've learnt so much French, haven't you?'

'Tons. Mostly rude words from Josette and romantic words from Philippe, and that's the useful kind of French, isn't it?'

'But I do miss Lily,' Ang said. 'I can't wait to see her. And my mum.'

I actually really didn't want to think about who I'm missing so I decided to try out what is widely known as the world's best distraction: dancing with a fit boy.

Philippe is a good dancer. With snogging skills to match.

It was a nearly perfect night, but I couldn't help sighing a bit when we got back to Josette's house.

LATER

I woke up in the middle of the night with a pain in my chest. I thought it might be Josette sitting on me, but then I realised that there was a Megs shaped hole inside me. I tossed and turned for a long time thinking about everything I said. Then I remembered some things that Megs said, like how the trip was a rip-off, and how I haven't seen her buy any new clothes this year, and how she said that they were saving up to send Grammy to Barbados in the summer.

The thing about stopping and thinking for a

minute, is that it can make you realise that you are an idiot. I shouldn't have gone on so much about Megs coming on the trip. And I shouldn't have taken it personally when she said no. I'm glad I'm going home soon because I really need to say sorry to Megs.

SATURDAY 26TH MAY

We went to Paris today. The Eiffel tower is pretty tall. It's a bit of a swizz though because you can't actually climb right to the top and straddle the little pointy bit, and swing out an arm and pretend you are King Kong on top of the Empire State Building.

Not that I was planning on doing that or anything.

What you can do get is your hair blown into a right old mess and then you have to attempt to look completely unfazed when French boys point and laugh at you and call out 'ourangutan!'. Which is actually the same word in French as it is in English. I can think of more useful words to keep the same like 'mascara' and 'crisps'.

Anyway, I'm pretty sure that they were calling me a big ginger monkey because I was covered in my own auburn hair, but it might also have had something to do with me trying out just a little bit of the King Kong business, using Josette as the pointy thing to swing on.

We also went to Notre Dame and the Musée d'Orsay. While I was admiring a Pissarro painting Icky said in her delightfully penetrating voice, 'This is rubbish. The people are all blobby. I could do better than that.'

'Wow, Vicky,' I said. 'I, for one, am delighted that you've managed to shake off that crippling shyness so that you're finally able to tell us what you really think.'

'It is rubbish, isn't it, Philippe?' she whined.

And Philippe said, 'The impressionists painters, they didn't want to show things how it is, they wanted to make it how you see things when you look at the crowd or the forest. You cannot take all the details, not every leaf or face, but you get an impression of colour and light.'

Uh huh. I snogged a really smart boy. 'Exactly,' I said. 'You can get an exact copy from a photo, this has got the feeling of the scene in it too.'

'Yes, yes!' Philippe said. 'Energy in the stroke of the brush.'

Even though Philippe is tall and Icky is the size of a malnourished gerbil she managed to look down her nose at him. 'I'll leave you two alone to your geek speak.'

Philippe looked at Icky as she walked off and then back at me.

'I'm thinking that also this Vicky is better

when she is far away and she is looking only like a blob.'

I told you he was smart.

SUNDAY 27TH MAY

This morning I had to say goodbye to the Josette family, which was very sad. I also had to say goodbye to Philippe, which was actually quite cheerful. He's lovely and we had a great time. He said that if I'm ever in France that I can come and stay with him. Since I'm going to combine being a prize-winning chemist with a few leading roles in blockbuster films, it seems obvious that I'll hardly be able to avoid being flown to Paris in a private jet now and then, so I'll definitely be seeing him again. When the bus drove away Josette chased after it waving for a couple of hundred metres. She is very silly (and surprisingly fast in those heavy boots) but I'm going to miss her a lot.

It seemed to take forever to get home. Even though I was sad to leave Josette and I had had a really good time I was sort of looking forward to seeing my idiot family again. Except Granny, maybe.

When we finally pulled into the school car park Mum, Dad and even Sam were there to meet me. I was so pleased I put Sam in a headlock.

'Ow! What are you doing that for?' he whined, as if he hadn't been pining for me all week.

'Because I'm happy to see you!'

'It hurts!'

'I can't help it if you can't tell the difference between my angry violence and my affectionate violence. Give it few more years and you'll get the hang of it.' And I twisted his ear in a loving fashion.

'Great,' he replied. 'Can I have my head back now? I'd like to bang it against a wall.' I released him and gave Dad a punch of joy.

Then Mum gave me a straight up cuddle. 'It's so nice to see you,' she said. 'Did you have a lovely time?'

I started telling them all about it. I still had plenty more to say by the time we pulled up at home, but as we were getting out of the car I remembered what was waiting for me. 'Is Granny here?' I asked.

'She's been here all week.' Sam scowled. 'And we've got two more to go.'

Mum tutted. 'Come on, Sam, it hasn't been that bad.'

Sam mouthed, 'It has.' And then he pulled a death-by-Granny face.

Inside, I found Granny in the kitchen. She greeted me with a cake, which is definitely my favourite way to be greeted. I looked down at the icing. In swirly letters it said WELCOME HOME FAI

'There's a bit missing!' I said.

Granny snatched the cake away. 'There's

gratitude. I see you haven't picked up any of that French elegance.'

I gave her my best scowl. 'Did you eat a slice?'

'They said you'd be back by six, it's half past now! I come over a bit funny if my blood sugar level drops.'

'So you ate some of my welcome home cake?'

'Yes and it's very good even if I do say so myself. Would you like a slice?'

I gave in and nodded. I wasn't going to quibble about a few missing letters when there was cake at stake.

It was quite tasty. If Granny could do a bit more baking and a little less meddling she'd be a passable house guest.

While I did the washing up after dinner and Granny pointed out what I was doing wrong, I asked her how her home improvements were coming along.

'It's lovely. I'm having magenta walls with pumpkin trim. My friend Keith is project managing – you remember Keith?'

It's hard to keep up with Granny's boyfriends. 'Is he the one who made a fortune in plastic cutlery?'

'No, he's the one with his own building company, so he's put his best men on it.'

'Does that mean it will be finished early?'

'Oh no, if anything it might take a bit longer. Keith's very thorough.'

I sighed. 'I don't know why you're bothering to redecorate at your age anyway. We'll only do it again when you're dead.'

Granny narrowed her eyes. 'That's the sort of attitude that has made me decide to leave my house to the cat.'

I flicked soap suds at her. 'You haven't got a cat.'

'If necessary, I will drag one off the streets. Even if it's the last thing I do.'

I dried my hands and helped myself to another slice of cake. 'I think you'll find that even cats object to a pink and orange kitchen.'

LATER

Since Granny has taken over my comfy bed, I have attempted to turn the lumpy old sofa into a cosy nest by covering it with all the cushions in the house. While I was settling down I remembered how furious Josette's mum was with Josette, until Josette's dad found out Icky had set us up. My mum would never have believed that the cigarettes were mine, even if I had said that they were. She would have known I was protecting someone.

It's nice to be home.

MONDAY 28TH MAY

There was no school today because of the bank holiday. I woke up early anyway because Granny was crashing about in the kitchen. I wouldn't have minded but when I called out a very polite request for her to make me a cappuccino with extra froth she called back something quite rude. Once I was awake, I started thinking about Megs. I want to see her but I know she's spending the day with her Grammy today. I could text her, but for the first time in my life I don't really know what to say.

I hate thinking she's cross with me; it's making me quite miserable. I barely even noticed the first two breakfasts I had.

I might have to try a third one.

LATER

While I was bravely working my way through another bowl of Coco Pops, my phone rang; when I saw it was Ethan my stomach did a double backflip. For one crazy moment I wondered if he had missed me while I was in France. Perhaps he was ringing to tell me that he prefers me to Dawn. When I finally managed to pick up and say, 'Hello?' in a rather wobbly voice he said, 'Hey Faith, can you do me a favour?'

I was fairly sure by this point that the favour wasn't to go on a date with him, so I was able to say, 'What sort of favour?' in a calmer tone.

'So my dad's friend is this multi-media type. I know it seems unlikely that my dad could have any cool friends, but I think that since he's been living with me some of my coolness has rubbed off on him. Anyway, his friend is setting up this teen website and he wants some video clips for the "friends" section.'

'Right.'

'And since I'm clearly a very cool teen he asked me if I could film one of my friends talking about mates. Just for a minute or two. I know that you and Megan aren't getting on well at the moment but I'm hoping you'll still do it.'

I sighed. It seemed like I couldn't escape thinking about Megs for five minutes. 'Well—'

'Go on, Faith, I need your help with this. And the whole project is due really soon, so do you think we could meet up? My house probably isn't the best idea so maybe the park?'

I wasn't entirely convinced by this video thing; since I played those tricks on Ethan last year I'm always a bit suspicious when he wants me to do something unusual. Is this all leading up to a practical joke? Maybe I should have said no, but the thing about Ethan is that he is pretty irresistible so I ended up agreeing. I'm going to be on my guard though.

LATER AGAIN

As soon as I walked in the park gates I could see Ethan by the swings. I walked towards him slowly scanning the trees and bushes just to make sure that there was no one waiting to pop out and ambush me, but when I reached him, the look on his face wasn't the cheeky twinkle of someone who is about to do mischief. Obviously, I'd been wrong to expect a practical joke.

'Thanks for coming,' he said. 'I appreciate it.'

I wanted to know why he hadn't asked Spawn, but I didn't want to bring her into the conversation so I said, 'How come you asked me?'

'Well ... my dad's friend has already got some footage of boys talking so he wanted a girl and he had a certain kind of girl in mind, you know? Energetic, pretty, relatable.'

I tried to hide my delight that Ethan thought that was a good description of me.

He got a tiny video camera out of his coat pocket and switched it on.

'What do I have to do?' I asked.

'Okay, maybe sit on the swing?' He touched my arm to guide me towards the swing. I was instantly covered in goose bumps.

'Then just look at the camera and tell me what's so great about your best friend.'

So he counted me in and I said, 'The thing I really love about my best friend Megs is that she's always there for me. She shares all my happy times with me and she looks after me when I'm miserable.

She even tells me when I'm wrong, which takes a really brave person.' Just thinking about Megsie was making me smile. 'With Megs, I feel like I've always got someone on my side and that's the best feeling.'

Ethan grinned at me. 'That was perfect. Brilliant. I know you two have had a bit of a bust up but it's obvious how well you get on really.'

I wanted to ask him if he'd seen Megs and if she'd said anything about me, but I was interrupted by his phone ringing.

'Just a sec,' he said and whipped out his phone. 'Hey, Dawn.'

My heart sank. There we were having a nice chat, why did she have to interrupt? I withdrew to the roundabout but I still heard enough to understand that he was late for meeting her. And that he was about to leave me.

He slid his phone back in his pocket.

'I've got to go, Faith,' he said.

'Sure.' I leant back and tried to give the impression that spending the morning pushing myself on the roundabout was definitely what I wanted to do.

'Westy's having everyone round his house this evening, can you come?'

'Um ... Does Westy actually want me there?'

'Of course he does. You two are still friends, aren't you?'

I shrugged. 'I hope so.'

'Seriously, Westy told me to ask you. He does want you there. We all do.'

His sparkly eyes looked so hopeful that I couldn't help saying, 'Okay then.'

'Brilliant. See you there.'

And he walked off across the park.

I went home to climb into my bed, but then I remembered Granny has taken over my bedroom, so I went into the dining room, closed the door behind me and lay on my cushion mountain. For three hours. Completely still. Except for my poor little heart which was burning and aching and turning itself inside out whilst shouting, *Stop stomping on me, Ethan!*

LATERER

When I finally pulled myself together, I got up and washed my face. I wasn't very hungry but I managed to choke down a triple decker sausage sandwich to stop me from fading away. I picked up my phone to call Megs, but then I put it down again. I want to talk to her, but I'm afraid she won't want to talk to me. Ethan said everyone is going to Westy's tonight, so maybe I'll just wait to see Megs there. That way I can work out if she hates me from a safe distance and if she does I can sneak off home and crawl under my cushions and cry.

Nice to have plans for the evening.

EVEN LATER

When I arrived at Westy's, Ethan opened the door.

'Hey,' I said.

'Hi.' He gave me a massive grin. In fact, he looked so pleased to see me that I sort of froze and just stood there smiling back at him.

He snapped out of it first. 'Er, so … Megan is here, but please don't get cross, I just want you to see something.'

He caught hold of my hand and pulled me into Westy's sitting room.

My hand.

He was holding my hand. I can only be thankful to my legs that they managed to keep going on auto pilot because the whole of my brain was given over to thinking about the hand situation. As we walked into the room, I caught sight of Megs who gave me a raised eyebrow. I don't know if the eyebrow was referring to the hand-holding or if it was some sort of greeting. I've told her before that her eyebrows need to learn to communicate more clearly. But before I could start wondering if Megs and her eyebrows were still mad at me, Ethan let go of my hand and said, 'Hit it, Westy.'

The lights went out and the TV went on. There on screen was my giant face. I mean, my head is normal sized (which is a miracle when you think about Dad's melon-head) but Westy's TV is huge.

Anyway, there it was, the video Ethan had made with me babbling on about how much I love Megs.

What the monkey was this all about? Then I got it. Ethan was staging some sort of intervention. I knew he was up to something! What a cheeky, presumptuous, completely and utterly lovely boy. I can't believe he went to all this bother just to help me and Megs out. How incredibly sweet. I turned to look at Megs who was wearing the expression she usually reserves for fluffy ducklings or when I let her have the last piece of cake. I think she liked hearing how ace she is. Then my head disappeared from the screen and we cut to Megs. Who had filmed her? And when?

Megs was chatting away in the 'special' voice that she uses when anyone films her. It's half cockney with a touch of American. 'My best friend is funny and smart and crazy good fun. Also, she tries really hard to hide it, but she is actually really kind. I know that whenever I need her she'll always look after me,' Megs said.

My heart squeezed. That girl is a Brussels sprout, but she really is the best. Suddenly I didn't feel worried or shy anymore.

'Oh, Megs!' I said pushing Elliot out of the way and flinging my arms around her.

Megs crushed me like a boa constrictor and lifted me off my feet.

The lights went back on and I realised that our whole gang was there cheering. They all knew about this! Sneaky chimps.

I looked around at my grinning mates. 'Whose idea was this?'

'Ethan's,' Cam said. 'Which is pretty surprising because usually he enjoys other people's misery.'

'Thank you,' I said to Ethan.

'That's all right.' I think he may have actually been blushing.

While everyone was getting into the crisps and fighting over the comfiest sofa, I pulled Megs out into the hallway.

'Listen, you and I know that I'm generally totally ace, but very occasionally I can also be a tiny bit bossy. I know I was being selfish trying to get you to come to France, but it's only because I love you and I like spending time with you. Even in crazy places like France.'

She nodded.

'I shouldn't have just assumed that you'd be able to afford to come with me. It was an expensive trip; my mum made a big thing of how I shouldn't expect much for Christmas. I'm sorry I wasn't more thoughtful.'

Megs let out a long breath. 'I probably wasn't completely fair. I mean, I don't think I would have liked it if you hadn't cared whether I came or not, it's just that … my parents are putting all their extra cash towards Grammy's visit to my Great Auntie's, so school trips aren't exactly the priority at the moment.'

'I should have known that.'

'Maybe I should have told you.'

'Maybe I should have given you a chance to tell me.'

She smiled and I felt a massive sense of relief.

'Sorry I was insensitive and that I tried to tell you what to do,' I said. 'I won't do it again.'

She punched me on the arm. 'Yes you will! But let's not fall out over it next time. I'll just put you in a half nelson until you stop it.'

'Fine. So we're back to being nice to each other, right?'

'That's right, fish face.'

'Nicer than that.'

And then she did put me in a half nelson, but it was quite a cuddly one.

We joined the others again and watched some more videos Ethan had made, including one of Cam attempting to jump off a shed and onto a wheelie bin. (The wheelie bin tipped up and he flew backwards into a hedge, but the best part of it was the way he just picked himself up and sauntered away as if nothing had happened.)

Westy wasn't exactly chatty with me, but half

way through the night he said, 'Do you want a crisp sandwich?'

I think we all know that you don't make a crisp sandwich for someone you hate, so that cheered me up.

'Is Dawn not coming?' I asked Ethan when I'd finished my sandwich.

He shook his head. 'Nah, she's doing her own thing.'

I couldn't help feeling pleased about this. 'I just wanted to say thanks again for setting me and Megs up – it was sweet of you.'

'Any time.' He looked at me, 'I don't like seeing you sad.'

It was tempting to mention at this point that if he really wanted to prevent any future sadness on my part then all he has to do is dump Dawn and ask me out. Two simple steps to get me perma-smiling.

'You and Megan are great together,' he went on. 'And Angharad's just been telling me how sweet you were to her in France. It's ace the way you look after your friends, Faith. Some girls, I mean, some people don't actually seem to care about their friends that much and just moan about them behind their backs. I think that if you're going to be mates you ought to be loyal.'

Oh my. Not only is he gorgeous and clever he is a really decent person.

He dropped the serious face. 'Of course, you've got to beat them up a bit and point out their minor imperfections in a hilarious fashion, just to keep them on their toes ...'

And he's funny. I was so full of swoony admiration at this point that I thought I might pop like balloon.

'... But you don't stab them in the back.'

'Exactly,' I agreed. 'That's one of the reasons I've never liked Icky. She ditches her so-called friends whenever they're not useful to her.'

'Uh huh.'

'Course, the main reason I hate her is because she squinted at me a bit once. When we were toddlers. On a very sunny day. But you can't expect a hatred of this sort of magnitude to be an entirely reasonable entity.'

He nodded solemnly. 'It's a once in a generation occurrence. We must respect your crazy-lady Icky-despising for its awesome depth and duration.'

I'd really missed chatting like this with Ethan. 'If only Miss Ramsbottom thought like you do. Instead it's all, "Stop giving the entire canteen an accurate report on which rotting vegetables Vicky smells like, Faith." And "Take those scissors out of Vicky's eyeball, Faith."'

He laughed and my middle did a loop the loop. 'She doesn't appreciate you,' he said.

'I know! If she'd j—'

'I do.'

That shut me up. Actually, it didn't. Because even though it seemed like he was saying that he appreciated me, I wanted to be absolutely clear, so I said, 'You do what?'

'Appreciate you.'

So then it was absolutely clear. He said it in this low voice while looking right into my eyes and I was looking right back at him, and I'd gone all floaty light because he *does* like me. Then I realised that this looking business had been going on rather a long time and, good gravy, it wasn't going to turn into kissing business was it? But then something terrible happened. Something truly revolting that should never happen to any girl on the possible-maybe verge of a kiss.

I heard my father's voice.

I don't mean in the room. He's been told that if he really has to interrupt me at a social gathering then he has to pretend to be a fireman evacuating the area. (And the face-covering breathing mask I have provided him with must be worn at all times.) Anyway, this hideous voice of my father was actually *in my head*. And it was repeating a bit of that conversation I had with him a few weeks ago, when I asked him if he thought Hypothetical Hannah could be friends with the boy she liked and he said: *Is this girl going to flirt with the boy?*. Oh no. This was terrible. I hadn't meant to flirt but now, here I was practically puckering up.

I took a step back from Ethan. 'Er, I, um,' I gabbled. 'I've got to get something to drink.'

He looked disappointed. Which is good. Because anyone who almost maybe nearly kisses me should be super sad when it doesn't happen.

Except, I'm quite glad it didn't happen. I don't want to kiss someone else's boyfriend.

What I want is for him to be my boyfriend and then we can snog until out lips fall off.

LATER

Why can't Ethan work that out for himself?

LATER STILL

Also, I could do without my dad roaming around my brain. Imagine what he might find in there.

TUESDAY 29TH MAY

Granny cooked us dinner tonight. I say 'cooked' but actually she just opened a jar of sauce and made Sam boil up a vast quantity of pasta.

'It's funny that you're making all this fuss about redecorating,' I said, when we all sat down tucking into this extremely bland feast. 'Because you're not much of a homemaker are you?'

Granny gave me one of her crocodile smiles. 'I've always found that people who visit my house are very glad they've done so.'

I shook my head. 'I think you're getting confused, what they're glad about is leaving.'

'Faith,' Dad said. 'Don't be so … cheeky.' I'm pretty sure that he almost said 'honest'.

I pouted. *'Don't be cheeky, don't flick over-cooked pasta at your brother*, what am I allowed to do?'

'You could try making polite conversation with your family.'

We all had a good laugh at that one.

LATER

I couldn't sleep because the sofa is so uncomfortable, so I got up and ate the rest of Granny's pasta. It wasn't that bad in the end. All it needed was a bacon sandwich on the side.

LATERER

Although Mum was quite stroppy about the perfectly acceptable late night activity of bacon frying. She thought I was a burglar.

I told her that if robbers get a bacon sandwich while they're on the job I am definitely adding that to my list of possible careers.

WEDNESDAY 30TH MAY

When I got home from school Sam was slumped at the kitchen table making the place look like a hostel for the unwashed and idiotic.

'What is it? Has Granny made you wash her tights?'

'No. She's out.' He groaned and clutched at his hair.

'I wouldn't do that if I were you,' I said. 'If Dad's anything to go by that mop will start falling out soon. If you give it a helping hand you'll be bald by the time you're nineteen.'

'I can't do it!' he moaned.

'Well, it's true being both stupid and bald is a bit of handicap, but Dad seems cheerful enough on it.'

He banged his head on the table. 'My homework, I can't do my stupid homework.'

I leant over his shoulder. He was supposed to be writing a letter from an evacuee to his parents.

'You're going about this all the wrong way, you aubergine,' I said helpfully. 'It's not about how much you write.'

'Isn't it?'

'Next you'll be telling me you're making your handwriting really big so that your words take up more space.'

He had the good grace to look embarrassed

'Listen, don't waffle. Teachers can spot waffle,

besides it just takes up their time to wade through it when really they'd rather be watching dog fights and drinking gin.'

'So what do you do?

'Find out what they want from you. Always ask what it is they want to see in your homework. Then you whack that in at the beginning. That way if their attention wanders while they're marking you'll still get credit.'

I looked at his homework sheet again. 'You're not being marked for your story writing here. What she needs is to see that you've actually learnt something about the Second World War and the evacuees. All teachers really want is some proof that you've been listening to them dribble on. It's quite sad really – their constant need for affirmation.'

I was feeling generous so I helped him bang out two paragraphs crammed with everything that he knew about evacuees. Which wasn't that much. But at least now he'll get credit for what his tiny brain managed to retain.

Sam grinned his wonky-toothed smile up at me. 'Thanks, Faith.'

'I'm not doing it for you. My reputation would be in tatters if anyone found out you don't know how to outsmart a teacher. Raise your game.'

He nodded hard.

It's a shame I've already decided to dedicate

my life to Science (or burglary). I think I'd make an excellent life coach.

THURSDAY 31ST MAY

I've been thinking about Ethan. I don't mean to, but he keeps popping up in my head like some sort of thought ninja. It was nice of him to care about me and Megs making up.

Really nice.

That's all I'm saying.

JUNE

FRIDAY 1ST JUNE

Miss Ramsbottom started today's assembly with what, I think, she thinks is a smile. It's not a real smile, she just stretches out her already thin lips until they almost disappear. She only ever does it when she wants something. I started calculating how many steps we were from the door and wondering if Ramsbum had any weapons concealed about her person.

She fixed us with her laser gaze. 'Today I want to talk about something that I know is very important to you all.'

I waited for her to start a nice chat about doughnuts or women's rights or something else that I can either eat or get enthusiastically shouty about. Instead, she told us how the school has taken great strides in becoming greener. It's not even true. They have the heating on in the summer and we've been asking for more recycling bins for ages. Although, the ICT department are quite strict about paper use; the teachers go nuts when you print out a really quite short magazine for just three hundred of your closest friends.

But I got the impression that suddenly Miss Ramsbottom was feeling very keen on the eco thing. It soon became clear why that was.

'This year,' she said. 'The Green Schools Alliance will be holding their conference here at Westfield

High, and as part of the proceedings there will be a presentation on the initiatives that we have set in place as a school. I am looking for girls to deliver the presentation and to act as school tour guides.'

Suddenly the entire hall was completely still. We all know that when Miss R is looking for victims it only takes an ill-timed fidget and you find yourself hauled off from your friends and made to sign your life away. I haven't forgotten when she made me 'volunteer' to wash bird poo off the head's car just because I tried to pass the time, during one of her super dull speeches on appropriate behaviour, by doing a very small amount of punching Lily in the head.

'I'm sure you're all keen to volunteer to represent your school.'

I concentrated on making myself invisible.

'I will place a signup sheet on the activities noticeboard and I look forward to seeing it full by the end of the day. Dismissed.'

But no one wanted to be the first to stand up just in case Miss R swooped down on them and took their names for her list. It took several minutes before I convinced the girls to make a break for the door.

At lunchtime, I was congratulating myself on having managed to avoid Ramsbum all day when Angharad said, 'Actually, I might sign up for the Green Schools thing.'

'Really?' Megs asked.

'I think the environment is important, don't you?'

Megs nodded. 'Of course, but I'm pretty sure that ozone layer will be just as happy with me in Juicy Lucy's as it would be with me sweating it out for Miss Ramsbottom.'

'I think the environment would actually be happier if we're happy,' Lily said through a mouthful of banana.

We all stared at her.

'Because Mother Nature always looks like that sort of person, doesn't she? Like she cares if you're happy.'

Before we could get any further into whether the environment is worrying about Lily's happiness levels, Ang said firmly, 'I like getting involved with things and I think it will be fun.'

Which made me wonder if perhaps I should spend more time reading Geography textbooks like Ang does, because then everything else really would seem super super fun. But what it comes down to is that Ang is my friend, and I always support my friends in their crazy ideas (and the fact that I point out their craziness and maybe even make them a t-shirt about it, is really only a formality).

'It's madness,' I said to Ang. 'But you can sign me up, if you want some company.'

'Me too,' Megs said.

Lily nodded her agreement.

Ang hesitated. 'Thanks, but you're just saying it to be nice, aren't you? You don't need to because I can definitely do this by myself.'

'But you don't have to,' I said.

Angharad swallowed. 'I'd like to.'

She seemed determined to stand on her own two feet so we didn't argue anymore. To be honest I was quite relieved because spending time with Ramsbum is asking a lot, even from a friend.

SATURDAY 2ND JUNE

Megs came over this afternoon while my parents were out shopping with Sam. Granny was at one of her carnival float meetings, so once we'd scoured the kitchen for snacks that weren't made of seaweed or tofu, we went upstairs to my room. Apart from a lingering whiff of Granny's old lady perfume, a peach cardigan and a load of sweet wrappers, my room seemed pretty much as I left it. Except for something black on the floor.

'Old people,' I said. 'So untidy. If she keeps this up, I'll dock her pocket money.' And then I did something really rash: I bent down and picked the thing up. Now, I've never really given much thought to my granny's underwear, but I suppose I had a vague sort of idea that she would wear a garment that covered that whole terrifying area completely. Something that went from waist to knees. Maybe

Victorian style bloomers. I never expected my granny's undergarments to be black and lacy.

Or in my hands.

As soon as I realised what I was holding I threw them away from me. Unfortunately, Megs had already settled herself on the bed and they landed on her head.

At first she didn't quite understand, she pulled them off her pony tail and opened them out.

'What the? Are these your granny's?'

I couldn't speak. I managed a bit of a blink.

'Please tell me they're clean.'

'I don't think even my crazy granny keeps her clean undies on the floor.'

'Gross!' Megs squealed, and she flicked the knickers away from her, towards me. I tried to bat them back, but they got stuck on my shirt button.

Megs yelped with laughter.

'Get them off me!' I shook from side to side, trying to dislodge them without actually handling them.

Megs was rolling around on the bed in hysterics.

'Megan Baptiste! Help me now!' I shouted, but she was no use at all. When you're facing a peril like this, you've really only got yourself to rely on; so I grabbed a pencil from my desk and managed to hook the knickers off my button and back in the direction of Megs. But she was too quick and scrambled away like a mad dog was coming at her. Which meant they landed on my pillow.

'Oh my God!' I gasped. 'Don't leave them there! I'll never be able to sleep again!'

'Do something Faith!'

So with remarkable bravery (and the sort of presence of mind that makes me wonder why the prime minister never phones me for advice), I wrapped my hand in Granny's cardi, picked up the knickers with my protected hand, stepped out on to the landing and threw the whole old lady pant-parcel on to Sam's bed. I closed his bedroom door and hopped back into my room.

Megs and I doubled over laughing and shaking and panting like two people who have just disposed of a hand grenade.

Eventually Megs started to say, 'I can't believe your granny wears a tho—'

'Stop right there!' I gripped her by the shoulders and stared into her eyes. 'We must never speak of this again. Understand?'

She nodded.

And then we tried to carry on like normal. Like people during the war bravely making a cup of tea in their bombed out kitchen.

But, to be honest, life will never be the same again.

Some things you just can't unknow.

SUNDAY 3RD JUNE

Lily rang me. 'What are you up to?' I asked.

'Arif came round yesterday to help me with my prepping.'

'Your prepping? What are you prepping for?' To be honest, Lily has never struck me as the sort of person that gets prepared for stuff. Normally, she just lets big things happen and then she does or says something crazy. Which is also what she does when nothing big has happened. When you think about it like that, she's actually a remarkably stable person.

'I'm prepping for a zombie apocalypse. Or an alien invasion. Or a plague of locusts. Basically, anything that's going to restrict my access to Marmite.'

'Right.' Always with the Marmite. I'm not saying it's not a tasty treat on toast, but it's not what I'd grab in an emergency.

'I started thinking that if something terrible happened there are a few things that I'd want to make sure I had.'

'I see, so what have you packed in your emergency bag?'

'Marmite.'

'Obviously. What else?'

'A mini vacuum cleaner. Because there won't be any power for the big one, will there? And a zombie mask – so I can blend in.'

'What if it's vampires not zombies?'

'I've got two Tic Tacs I can tape to the zombie mask mouth for fangs.'

'Have you got some sort of locust costume?'

'I decided locusts are probably scared of zombies.'

'Uh huh.' I was starting to wish I had some chocolate to get me through this conversation. 'What else?'

'A bass recorder.'

'A recorder? One of those instruments that they made us squeak out Hot Cross Buns on at primary school?'

'Yep, but a bass one.'

I snorted. 'Because an ordinary one wouldn't do?'

'Well, you *can* knock someone out with one of the little ordinary ones, but, as I'm sure you know, it's much quicker and less tiring to the arm muscles if you use a big bass one.'

I thought we should move on from my familiarity with the relative effectiveness of various instruments as weapons so I said, 'Is that it?'

'Finger paints, salad tongs and a chocolate Santa.'

'Sounds great.'

'Yep, I'm pretty pleased.'

There was a pause where I could almost feel Lily's satisfaction radiating down the line. She's clearly going to sleep well tonight.

'Hey Lils,' I said. 'I've been meaning to ask you about Angharad. Is she really okay about doing this Green Schools thing by herself?' Normally, Ang is so timid about talking to people she doesn't know well.

'I think so. Now we're getting a bit older she's trying hard to build up her confidence. She doesn't want her shyness to hold her back.'

I hadn't realised that Ang had been thinking about all this. 'So you don't think we should do Green Schools?'

'Nah. We love Ang so much that we always want to help her and look after her but I reckon the best thing we can do is to let her have the opportunity to stand on her own two feet.'

This was a good point but I was so surprised that Lily had made a good point that it took me several seconds to get my mouth to say, 'Good point.'

'Mmm, that's why I didn't go to France. She was scared to go without me but I wanted her to know that she can do anything she wants.'

Wow. Lily had taken my breath away. First zombie death by bass recorder and then this remarkably insightful and kind attitude towards Angharad. 'Lily, how do you manage to be both loopy and brilliantly perceptive at the same time?'

'Dunno,' she said. 'Maybe it's all the Marmite I eat.'

MONDAY 4TH JUNE

I love half term. I even like waking up at the normal time just so I can enjoy going back to sleep. I think they should give us quarter terms too.

Good job I've been getting plenty of sleep though, since Granny kept me up late last night. After dinner she announced, 'I've got to make some tissue paper flowers for the carnival float. I need them for tomorrow.'

Mum stared at her, but Granny went on unabashed. 'I expect you'd all like to help?'

Mum stopped staring and started clearing away dishes. Sam and I looked at our plates and Dad actually got under the table and started scraping up that sticky green stuff that's been there all week.

'Come on! Who will help?'

'Why haven't you mentioned this before?' Mum asked.

I shot Granny an almost sympathetic look, this is the kind of shrieky response I get when I politely ask for art supplies for a project on Mexico a full twelve hours before it's due in.

'I've been busy,' Granny said. 'But I must get them done tonight because I promised, and if I don't come up with the goods I'll never hear the end of it from Mrs Moore.'

Mum tutted. 'The children have been lounging

around the house all day. You could have got them helping then. It will be Sam's bedtime soon.'

Granny shook her head. 'I couldn't fit it in earlier, I had a lunch date.'

'Some things are more important than romance,' Dad said from under the table.

Granny eyed Dad's backend. 'Well, we all know that's your attitude.'

Mum scowled. 'Insulting my husband isn't going to make me more likely to help you out of the mess you've got yourself into.'

That sentence sounded familiar. Except when I hear it she says 'insulting your father'. I was actually starting to feel quite sorry for Granny so I said, 'I'll help.'

Dad backed out from under the table. 'Marvellous. That's that solved then. What a great opportunity for Faith to improve her, er, helping skills. I expect you'll want to work out here in the kitchen. The light's very poor in the sitting room. We'll just shut ourselves in there with the TV and the scotch and keep out of your way.'

And they were gone. All three of them skedaddled off without a backward glance. In the hallway I heard Mum say, 'There's nothing wrong with the light in here, is there?

And Dad said, 'There will be when I get the bulb out.'

That was the last we heard from that shirker.

As the only responsible, kind-hearted member of my family I pushed Granny out of my favourite chair and said, 'Right then, let's get started. How many flowers have we got to do?'

'Five hundred.'

'Good grief! Couldn't you have enlisted your army of gentlemen friends to help?'

She smiled. 'Who do you think made the first five hundred?'

Which just goes to show that she's not as helpless as Mum makes out.

'This is what you do, Faith.' And she showed me how to pleat the tissue paper, trim the ends and tie it in the middle. 'Then you fluff it out and ... ta dah!'

It really was quite a sweet little flower. We only needed 499 more.

So we folded and snipped and fluffed and folded some more. It was quite fun to begin with. Then the hand cramp set in. I started getting a bit sloppy with the scissors.

'Steady on!' Granny snapped when one of my petals ended up a bit spiky. 'We want blossoms not cactuses.'

'It's cacti,' I said.

'Actually it can be either, but we want neither. You'd better stop and make the tea.'

Honestly, you do one extremely large favour for the woman and she just wants more, more, more.

I made the cup of tea anyway. To Granny's credit she didn't even pause to sip, she said, 'Fetch me a straw!' and with that she managed to drink tea and carry on with the flower folding. She's quite stubborn when she wants to be.

I found that by putting two whole biscuits in my mouth at the same time I could keep snipping and take on vital sugar at the same time.

Granny eyed at the biscuit plate. 'Feed me a biscuit,' she said.

'Granny,' I said, spraying a fair amount of bourbon crumbs in her direction. 'I know you're getting on and obviously you've got some sort of false teeth issues that I can't even bring myself to think about too much, but I'm pretty sure that you can still manage a bit of biscuit crunching. Suck it if you have to, just don't make any slurpy noises. I get enough of that from Megs and Cameron.'

'I don't need you to chew it for me, I'm not a baby bird.'

She's not a baby anything.

'I just want you to put it in my mouth. My hands are busy.'

It was true, even being a bossy old witch wasn't slowing her production line.

Anyway, I poked a biscuit into her mouth and

managed to avoid getting any granny dribble on me.

On and on we went. Granny babbled on about what a smug-chops Mrs Moore is and I really did want to help Granny get one over on her, but my fingers were getting stiff and slowing me down.

At ten o'clock I stopped to count. I was a good deal more depressed when I found out how many more we had to go.

Mum appeared in the doorway. 'Gosh, you've done well,' she said. 'Are you nearly there?'

'No!' Granny and I barked together.

Mum looked at her watch. 'You might have to finish in the morning.'

'I've got to deliver them at eight,' Granny said waving the scissors about as if I've got eyes to spare.

'Oh. Well, I do think it's time Faith went to bed,' Mum said.

To be honest I was ready to put my head down on the piles of flowers, but I kept on chopping. 'I can't go to bed,' I said. 'She hasn't finished.'

'That's your grandmother's problem. She shouldn't have left her homework to the last minute.'

'Is she always this unsupportive?' Granny asked.

'It's not her fault,' I said. 'She doesn't understand our creative clocks.'

Mum tsked. 'Creative clocks? More like last minute loonies.'

Granny sat up tall. 'I'll make sure that Faith has adequate rest.'

'Fine.' Mum shut the door while muttering to herself.

'Adequate rest?' I asked Granny.

'You don't need more than two or three hours do you? If I had your young body I could run the country and still have time for caravan holidays and jazzercise.'

In the end we actually finished just after midnight.

'Phew!' I said. 'Next time you've got a project on you can leave me out of it. Unless it's some sort of cake eating marathon. I could really help you shine there.'

'Don't tell your mother how late we stayed up.' Granny pulled me to my feet. 'Thank you, Faith. I could never have got them all done without you. In fact, while we've been working, I've been thinking ...' she twisted her mouth in an effort to get the words out. 'You're not a complete disappointment to me.'

I raised my eyebrows. 'Thank you Granny, and I'll take this opportunity to tell you that your nightmarish behaviour is not entirely unremitting. Overall, you're not a bad old bag of bones.' I yawned. 'Now that we've opened our hearts I think we'd better get to bed before Mum grounds us both.'

TUESDAY 5TH JUNE

Granny has been swanning about with a smug look on her face. Mrs Moore was late to the float decorating session and when she did get there she hadn't made as many flowers as Granny. We got to hear all the smart remarks she made about Mrs Moore not keeping her promises. She's actually quite funny when she's being mean.

She must be picking up a few hints from me.

WEDS 6TH JUNE

I went into town with the girls to meet up with the boys. Ethan was in really good form; taking the mickey out of everyone. In fact, I was pretty funny myself. At one point, I did my best impression of Icky and Ethan gave me a high five. I couldn't help thinking about what it would be like if we were going out, and cracking jokes together. We'd have a great time. Shame he's got someone else to do a double act with. Although, I couldn't help noticing that Dawn wasn't with him.

Later, while we were sat by the fountain having a milkshake, Westy shuffled over and sat down next to me. I haven't had a good chat with him in ages. Looking at him with his two milkshakes and a four pack of muffins, I felt really sad that things have been weird so I said, 'All right, Westy?' and I really meant it.

He nodded and I thought he meant it too. I wanted to say something about everything that had happened, but I didn't want to make him uncomfortable so I just said, 'Everything ... all right then?'

'Yeah, yeah, I mean ... you know how sometimes things are a bit not all right, but then you stop being dopey and it's all all right again?'

I sort of understood. 'Uh huh.'

Westy put down his snack and ran his crumby hands through his hair. 'So ... yeah, I'm all right. Are you all right?'

'I am,' I smiled. 'I feel more all right knowing you're all right, because you know I think you're great, don't you?'

Then he gave me a bear hug that has probably displaced a number of my internal organs.

THURSDAY 7TH JUNE

Granny has been locked in my room all day working on her costume for the carnival.

There are some things that I enjoy about the carnival (candyfloss, the floats that throw out sweets, the fairground rides) and there are other things I don't enjoy. Mostly, Granny's carnival costume. Every year, she manages to choose an incredibly inappropriate outfit. I've suggested over and over again that she really embraces the carnival spirit and goes for one of those costumes that completely covers you – like a tree. Or the back end of a horse, but she always ignores my good advice in favour of more spangly options. I don't like to think about what she's going to come up with this year.

It can't possibly be worse than the time she was on an Arabian Nights float and went as a belly dancer.

FRIDAY 8TH JUNE

You'd expect a witty, intelligent, attractive girl like me to have plenty of invitations on a Friday night, wouldn't you? Actually, I only had one, it was from Granny. She said, 'You've got a face like a spanked behind. Why don't you pretend to be a normal person instead of a teenager and make some polite conversation? If you're good I'll let you help me sort my pills out.'

Granny takes a million vitamins and supplements. Every Friday she sorts them all out into a box with little compartments with days of the week on them so that she knows what to take when, and doesn't get confused. Personally, I think she needs more than a plastic box to stop her doing daft things.

I sat down with only a small amount of groaning and started reading pill bottles to stop myself from strangling Granny with one of Mum's dreamcatchers.

'Why do you take all this stuff anyway?' I asked.

'Keeps me fit and healthy.' She beamed at me with her false teeth and her wrinkly face.

'Whoa, imagine what you'd be like without them. It would be like one of those films when the mummy comes to life and crawls out of the tomb and its face is all mouldy and its arm is hanging off.'

'Don't be rude. When you're my age you'll count yourself lucky if you're in such good shape as I am.'

Just to prove Mrs Webber wrong when she says I can't control my mouth, I didn't say anything about Granny's shape. Which is roughly the shape of a pear. One that's been in the fruit bowl so long that no one wants to eat it, but no one wants to put it in the bin either because they're worried if they touch it, it might be all mushy on the bottom. That sort of shaped pear.

When we finished our exciting pill-based task I let Granny talk me into playing cards with her. She taught me poker then I taught her Scabby Queen. The best thing about Scabby Queen is that you get to pinch the loser's hand with your finger nails, which means that even if your opponent is super annoying you can still have a good time.

We'd just opened our third family-sized bag of popcorn when Mum came in.

'You two look like you're enjoying yourselves.'

Granny and I scowled at each other.

'What are you playing?' Mum asked.

'Scabby Queen,' Granny said.

Mum frowned at me. 'I don't think you should be playing that violent game with your grandmother.'

'But she loves violence!'

'I know. But she's an old lady and I'm not sure it's good for her to have you attacking her hands like that.'

'Don't be stupid, she hardly even bleeds.'

Granny nodded in agreement, but she didn't say anything because she was taking advantage of me being distracted by Mum's wittering and cramming her mouth with more than her fair share of popcorn.

Mum shook her head. 'I'm not sure that's a good thing.'

'I'll go gently on her.'

Which was a lie. If you show an enemy like Granny a little kindness, they'll have your head off before you know it.

SATURDAY 9TH JUNE

Today was the carnival. When Granny came downstairs she said, 'It's a shame your little French friend doesn't arrive till next Saturday. I'm sure she would have enjoyed today's festivities.'

I looked Granny up and down; she was wearing a very small dress and a very big hat. 'Yes, I'm sure she would have found it all very amusing,' I said. 'What are you wearing? Is that your costume?'

'Of course it's not my costume!'

'Oh, silly me, can't think why I thought you were in fancy dress. Maybe it was those feathers on your head? But I expect I'm a little behind the times. No, wait, I am a teenager and at the forefront of fashion, so I'll stick with my original thought, what on earth are you wearing?'

Granny struck what she thinks is a model pose. 'I always look tasteful whether I'm keeping it casual in nautical slacks or dressing up in sequins.'

'Hmm. You do know that most old ladies' idea of getting dressed up is a fresh pair of tights and a nice floral top from Marks and Spencer?'

'Thank you Faith, when I get old, I'll bear that in mind.'

She stroked the purple velvet of her dangerously short skirt. 'Anyway, you wouldn't want me to look dull, would you?'

Which just goes to show that she doesn't listen to a word I say, because I have asked her repeatedly if she could try looking dull. Like a proper grandma. But I managed to keep my thoughts to myself because I didn't want her to change her mind about giving me a lift into town. When she dropped me off I said, 'Good luck with your float.'

'Thank you Faith, I'm sure our flowers will look marvellous.'

'Listen, when they're announcing the winners, just remember one thing will you?'

'What's that?'

'We don't like losers in this family. If you fail you can sleep on the floor tonight.'

'I won't fail.' And she bared her dentures in an impressively aggressive fashion. I'm amazed she hasn't had them sharpened into fangs.

I found Megs, Cam, Ang, Elliot, and Westy under the clock tower as arranged. Ethan and Lily were late.

'Is Dawn coming?' I asked Westy in a super casual fashion.

'Don't think so. They don't, you know, go everywhere together all the time.'

I couldn't help being a tiny bit pleased.

When Ethan turned up five minutes later I tried not to notice that he was looking rather nice. He was wearing a pale blue t-shirt. I'm not used to seeing him in light colours. It made him look sort of softer. I found myself staring at the point where his arm came out of the sleeve. I wanted to push back the fabric and touch his shoulder.

We walked through town and positioned ourselves near the end of the float route, where it was less crowded.

'Best spot for making sarcastic remarks,' Ethan said to me. 'By the time they get here hopefully half their float will have blown away and the carnival princesses will be pulling each other's hair.'

'That's a bit of a stereotype,' I said. 'I'm sure carnival princesses are quite capable of sorting out their differences in a civilised fashion.'

'Like you do?' he asked.

'Yep. And we all know that that means a sensible discussion followed by a swift wallop to anyone who still disagrees with me.'

The sun was out, but it was pretty windy. I hoped that whatever Granny's costume was made of, that it was strong enough to hold up to a stiff breeze.

The first float came round the corner. It had some sort of love theme and was covered in hearts and flowers in a bewildering range of pinks, reds and oranges.

'Wow,' Ethan said. 'That's eye-catching.'

'Mmm hmm, definitely feels like they've caught my eyes. On fish hooks.'

'Look.' Ethan pointed back at the float. 'They're dancing.'

The three middle aged couples on the float were attempting a tango.

He grimaced. 'I hope the next float is an ambulance one. I can hear their backs cracking from here.'

The wind was whipping about making my eyes water. I wiped at them.

'Is that a tear of joy?' Ethan asked. 'Are you moved by the spectacle, Faith?'

I smacked him on the arm. 'Actually, their wrinkly grinding has ruptured my already damaged eyes and now I've got eyeball fluid running down my cheeks.'

He snorted. 'You're funny.'

Which I knew was a huge compliment coming from him. 'Thanks. You should try cracking a few jokes yourself, instead of being so serious and polite all the time.'

He grinned at me. 'Faith, I know we've had our ups and downs but I just wanted t—'

'Yoo-hoo! Faith!' someone bellowed from a passing float.

I froze.

Obviously, it was Granny interrupting what was clearly something very important and heartfelt that Ethan was about to say.

I turned round and the theme of Granny's float was revealed in all its terrifying glory: Hawaii.

I knew this immediately because Granny was wearing a hula skirt.

And not much else.

If anyone else's grandparents wear skirts made of grass and a cropped t-shirt that says 'I'll have a pina colada' I'm pretty sure that they only do it at appropriate times such as on a tropical island several thousand miles away, or thirty years before their grandchildren are born.

'Cover your eyes!' I said to Ethan, but this only made him stare even harder to see what I was shrieking about. I put myself between him and the float, but despite what Icky says about the size of my hips there were only so many beach-ready geriatrics I could block from his view.

Granny was waving at Ethan.

And he was actually waving back. 'Your grandma's great.'

'She's a great something. Idiot is the word that comes to mind.'

'But your family get along, don't they?'

'That's not exactly how I would describe it.'

'You spend time together. I think that's brilliant.'

Granny was blowing him kisses. Then she spotted Westy, who she's got a real soft spot for and she threw him her garland of flowers. Fortunately, the float finally passed us before she could whip off anything else and lob it at a crowd of strangely amused teenage boys.

'She always has fun though, doesn't she?' Ethan laughed. 'I like that. That's what I like about you too.'

So it would seem that Spawn is Ethan's favourite girl closely followed by my own grandmother while I limp in third. Marvellous.

LATER

We had some chips and sat in the park until it got dark enough to enjoy the funfair. I don't know why they don't keep the waltzers on the green all year round. It would liven things up a bit. There was a really good atmosphere. I think it was because everybody was so happy that it hadn't rained.

'Do you want to go on that?' Lily asked and she pointed at a ride called Chaos that was like a giant arm with a carriage on, that swung back and forth, higher and higher, until eventually you went right over the top.

Megs sucked in her breath 'I don't know, I'm not that keen on heights.'

'I am,' Ang said, her face all lit up, 'I love them. I'll go on it. What about you, Faith?'

'Yep, come on.'

It was like my brain was pressing up against one side of my skull and then the other.

It was brilliant.

After that we all went on the ghost train. The carriages only held two people and somehow I ended up sitting next to Ethan.

'You can hold my hand if you get scared,' he said. 'But not my right hand, that's my stabbing hand. If an army of the undead come for us, I'm going to need that.'

'Yeah, that will be useful just as long as you can

get your trembling legs to work,' I said, but I was mostly thinking about what he'd said about holding his hand. Was he in the market for some hand holding? Had he finally got tired of Dawn's hands? Which while being very attractive and good at playing the drums and all, are clearly not the perfect hands for him.

The carriage was pretty small. While we were waiting for everyone else to get in I realised that my thigh was just touching Ethan's thigh. I was pretty sure that we hadn't started off like that when we first sat down. Did that mean he'd shifted closer to me? Or maybe I'd done it without noticing. Either way, neither of us moved apart. So there we were, staring ahead with our legs touching.

The ride clunked into life and set off towards some luminous dancing plastic skeletons. Up in front I could hear Cam pretending to have hysterics.

A clammy hand stroked my hair.

'Ew! What the hell?' I realised even as I was saying it that it was part of the ghost train and must have been made of rubber or something, but it still felt disgusting. I wiped at my forehead with my sleeve.

'Are you scared?' Ethan asked, obviously entertained by my squealing.

'Stop laughing at me! It was just that gross hand.'

'What this one?' And I felt a tap on my right

shoulder. 'I thought it was looking good. I've only just had a manicure.'

'Very f— Oh!' a lit up coffin burst open and a dummy sat up.

'You *are* scared!

Before I could explain that in my house if you don't jump when you see a sudden movement you'll end up with a fork in your eye, he said, 'Ah, poor girl.'

And then he put his arm around me.

He honestly did. My heart started to gallop and my stomach went skittering after it. My skin was zinging.

I didn't know what to do, then he said, 'Faith.'

And I turned to look at him, I could just about see his face in the green light coming from a witch's cauldron. I didn't breath. His eyes dipped just for a second to my mouth and ...

'OH MY GOD, IT'S A GIANT RAT!'

We jerked away from each other and Ethan swiftly removed his arm.

In the half light in front of us, the gigantic shadow of Westy loomed up, pointing into the darkness. 'Who saw that?' he shouted. 'That was real! It was the size of a Labrador! Seriously, they could put that in a show.'

Westy kept on about mutant rodents for the rest of the ride while I tried to get my breathing under control.

Ethan didn't say anything. When we came back out into the fresh air he couldn't get out of the carriage fast enough.

We went on a lot more rides and Westy ate a lot more hot dogs but Ethan didn't sit next to me again. When it was time to go and meet our various lifts, Ethan just said a general 'See you,' and disappeared.

I didn't even get to talk to Megs about it because her Mum was giving Cam a lift home too.

What the hell has happened? Did I almost kiss Ethan – again? What was I thinking? What was he thinking? And most of all, why did the tiny dad in my head not have anything to say about it?

I'm confused.

Really confused.

SUNDAY 10TH JUNE

I woke up early this morning and went straight round to Megs to tell her about Ethan. Although, after thinking about it all last night I was starting to wonder if there was actually anything to tell.

'What sort of way did he put his arm around you?' Megs asked.

'I don't know. Maybe it was just a jokey way because he thought I was being such a scaredy-cat?'

'Yeah, but even jokey arms-aroundsies mean something.'

'Do they?'

'Definitely. What did you think was going to happen before big mouth Westy started bellowing?'

'Well, it kind of seemed like *something* was going to happen. But I'm starting to think I was imagining it.'

'He likes you.'

I'm not so sure. 'Anyway, he's got a girlfriend, so until he does the decent thing and tells her that their relationship was a horrible mistake, I wouldn't kiss him even if he tried.'

I had lunch at Megs's house and then headed off.

MONDAY 11TH JUNE

Granny left today. I've had my window open all day and the smell of Yardley Lace perfume has finally subsided from vomit-inducing to just eye-watering. By the time I leave home it might have disappeared completely.

LATER

I wouldn't say that I exactly miss Granny. It's just that when I play Scabby Queen with Sam or Dad they end up crying. I can't wait for Josette to arrive. I bet she can take a pinch or seventeen.

TUESDAY 12TH JUNE

This evening I was spending my time profitably by rolling around on the sofa wondering what Ethan will say to me at debating tomorrow and if it might be *You're the loveliest girl in the universe, please go out with me*. Then Mum took one look at me and insisted I looked droopy, so she dragged me off to visit her cousin's daughter who has just had a baby.

Once she'd wrestled me into the car, I said, 'I'm hardly even related to this child, why do I have to go and look at it?'

'Be nice, Faith. Everybody loves babies.'

'Listen, I would probably be just as delighted by tiny chubby cheeks as the next person if you hadn't given me aversion therapy in the form of Sam.'

'Don't be mean about your brother.'

I flipped through her rubbishy CD collection. 'I'm just stating the facts. Remember his nappies?'

'Well, he was a little late to potty-train.'

I gave up on trying to find a CD that wasn't whale music or folk rock and switched on the radio. 'Those nappies were toxic. I'm surprised the council didn't ask you to stop putting them in the bin and provide you with one of those special barrels that they seal nuclear waste in.'

Mum tutted. 'He was a sweet little boy. You used to enjoy playing with him.'

'Yeah, that was until he stopped letting me saddle him up and ride him around the garden. It makes me sad to think that anyone related to me would let a small thing like a broken ankle stop them from affording their big sister fun and transportation.' I shook my head in disappointment. 'Such weak bones. I blame your side of the family.'

Mum frowned and because my one weakness is how much I care about people, I took pity on her.

'We did used to love playing pirates,' I said. 'And ninjas, and fire-breathing monster robots.'

'Yes, it was a rough time for my ornaments.'

'Listen, that pagan goddess china figurine looked a lot better after she'd commanded a platoon of Barbies in the garden. The pagans loved mud, didn't they? Isn't that why hippies don't wash?'

Mum rolled her eyes. 'Still, you two did have a lot of fun didn't you?'

Actually, now that I think about it, we did.

We also broke a lot more stuff than my mum realises. Most of it is buried in the garden. It's the reason I had to make strenuous objections to my dad's plans for a vegetable patch last summer.

Anyway, I hope the brattling that we went to see today gets a sibling. Everyone should have a little brother or sister to beat up, or play with, depending on their mood.

Mum came over all soppy on the way home. She kept saying, 'Wasn't she lovely?'

'I'm not saying I wasn't impressed by her ability to put her own foot in her mouth, or the way she dribbled enough to soak through three bibs in an hour, but I'm not sure that "lovely" is the word I'd choose.'

She wasn't listening. 'Sometimes I think …'

'Sometimes you think what? That a woman of your age should stop wearing vest tops?'

'No.'

'That if you gave up all this New Age shop nonsense and got yourself a nice steady cleaning job and really buckled down to it, you could afford to buy me a car when I'm seventeen?'

'Never mind.' And she shook her head. She does that a lot when she doesn't want to face the truth.

Later on I saw her showing dad the photos of the baby she took on her phone and making cooing noises.

Honestly. She needs a hobby.

WEDNESDAY 13TH

I was a bit nervous by the time we got to debating club this afternoon. I wasn't sure how Ethan was going to act towards me after the whole thing at the carnival. But when he got there he just said, 'All right, Faith?' and started telling everyone a funny story about his maths teacher's socks. He was behaving like nothing had happened. I was a bit disappointed.

After the debate, we ended up walking down the stairs together and he gave me this funny, slightly disapproving look and said, 'I hear you had a good time in France.'

At the time, I was absolutely convinced that from the way he said 'good time' that someone had told him about Philippe and that was what he was referring to. But now I know that I read way too much into it. Anyway, somehow I felt like maybe the only thing that was stopping him from dumping Dawn and asking me out was because he thought that I was involved in a cross-channel romance. Now that I'm writing it down, it seems like a ridiculous idea, but it honestly made sense to me then. Which is why I launched into a long rambling speech:

'Yeah, France was good. I've been thinking though. You know how sometimes you meet someone and they're great and everything, and you get along really well and you have a good time, but ultimately, in the end, for whatever reason, you know that things aren't going to last.'

He was watching me with a strange expression on his face.

'Um, so I don't know, I think it's probably best to be honest with yourself about where a relationship is going and, you know, make a clean break and then mayb—'

'What the hell, Faith?'

I was already regretting opening my mouth. 'I mean ...'

'You have a strop because I told you what I thought about you hurting Westy's feelings and now you're telling me Dawn's not good enough. You're such a hypocrite!'

Oh no. Oh no, no, no. He thought I was telling him to split up with Dawn. 'That's not what I meant. I wasn't talking about Dawn. Honestly, Ethan I—'

'Forget it Faith, I'm sick of people trying to twist what they've said. Just leave it.'

And he strode off out the gates.

I'm such an idiot. Why did I even try to explain about Philippe? I mean, Ethan clearly doesn't even care. Besides, why shouldn't I have a romance? And where does Ethan get off thinking everything is always about him. I'm not even going to ring him; I've got nothing to apologise for.

THURSDAY 14TH JUNE

I had to put Ethan out of my head today because this afternoon it was our key stage four assembly. We only get one a term and it's a wonderful opportunity for us all to catch up on the exciting activities going on in other years. At least that's how Miss Ramsbottom introduced it. Actually, it's usually a wonderful opportunity to catch up on some sleep while the Year Elevens ramble on about how hard they've been working, but today I had to give my report on the French exchange and I thought it might be best for everyone if I, at least, stayed awake during it.

So there I was sitting on stage knowing that this was my shot at getting Miss Ramsbottom's support for my prefect application. Eventually, the athletics club stopped trying to make seventeenth place out of eighteen schools sound like a good thing and Miss R introduced me. I stood up very tall and wished I'd worn some glasses so I could peer over them in a scholarly fashion.

'Last month, thirty Year Tens travelled to the South West of France as part of our exchange programme with Lycee Louis Lumiere.' My voice sounded kind of small in that big hall, which is strange because I have only ever heard my voice described as loud. I remembered what Granny said about opening the back of the throat and projecting into the audience (and she's an expert, her voice can penetrate several layers of duvet wrapped around my head). 'Visiting France was a superb opportunity to experience real-life French. I ordered hot chocolate in a café, bought baguettes in the boulangerie, and asked them to bring me a much larger cake in the patisserie.' I paused for effect. 'I even spoke French in situations entirely unrelated to food.'

Everybody laughed. I relaxed a bit and stopped worrying about what my throat was doing and it managed all by itself, which is the usual arrangement we have, so I should probably stick with that.

'We were also fortunate enough to enjoy several cultural experiences in France. We were bathed in colour at the Musée d'Orsay and surrounded by history at Notre Dame.

I highly recommend participating in an exchange programme to anyone who has the opportunity. Being immersed in the French language really helps to reinforce all the French that you know and helps you to pick up even more. Basically, you've got a week long opportunity to practice your skills with a personal tutor. Also, hearing so much French has really helped my accent. Overall, I'm sure that this trip has improved my French and hopefully it will contribute to a high grade in my French GCSE next year.

Added to that, the nicest part of my trip was getting to know my host, Josette, and her family. This trip has given me education, stimulation and, most importantly, a friend for life.'

I got a big clap. I mean, everyone in those assemblies gets a clap because people are afraid that if they don't applaud, Miss Ramsbottom will jab them in the neck with her fountain pen, but usually people's hands are clapping while their faces are telling you to make next term's report on the knitting club a lot shorter. But I like to think that people were doing proper clapping for me. Lily definitely was. She used her hands, her feet and the heads of the girls in the row in front of her to make appreciative noises.

Anyway, Miss Ramsbottom didn't clap herself. (I don't think she can, she's had all the joy and happiness sucked out of her, so now she's basically dusty bones. If she slapped her hands together hard I'm pretty sure they'd snap off at the wrists.) But she did give me a little nod. A nod is a 'yes' isn't it? So this must mean she's going to endorse my prefect application.

LATER
Chatting about France has reminded me of how brilliant Josette is. Once she arrives on Saturday, I'll be too busy laughing to worry about Ethan. I can't wait for her to meet Megs and everyone. Obviously, they'll love her because she's basically me, but French. And I think their depth of admiration for me is probably enough to make up for the Frenchness.

FRIDAY 15TH JUNE
Today started off ordinarily enough but nothing could have prepared me for the shock I got this evening. There I was, the picture of teenage good behaviour, doing the washing up after having only been asked a mere six times, when Mum announced: 'Gemma's baby made me think, perhaps we'll have another one.'

'Another what?' I asked.

'Baby.'

I had a nasty feeling about this. 'What do you mean a baby?'

'You know, another child.'

The horrible truth of what she was saying sunk in. 'You can't have a baby! You'd be old enough to be its grandmother! You'd pick it up and it'd be looking over your shoulder for its real mum.'

'I'm forty, Faith. Lots of women have babies in their forties.'

'Lots of women in their forties wear jeggings. It doesn't mean it's a good idea.'

'Wouldn't you like a little brother or sister?'

I looked at her. 'I've got a little brother and I don't like him.'

'I know you two row and mess about but—'

'I don't like him. Although, if you had another one I suppose I could pit them against each other in a sort of gladiator type situation.'

Mum sighed. 'Maybe we should discuss this when you've had a bit of time to think about it.'

Time to think about your parents making a baby is something no one needs

SATURDAY 16TH JUNE

Lovely Josette is here. Lovely, crazy, noisy Josette is here in my house.

Did I mention she's crazy?

She was the first off the bus, a whirl of hair and balloons. Yep, balloons. She brought me a bunch of balloons all the way from France. What a sweetie.

When we got back home I was showing Josette how, if you put Mum's mini exercise trampoline in the middle of the sitting room, you can get from the doorway to the sofa to the bookcase to the sideboard, all without touching the ground. Then Sam came back from football – he looked from me to Josette and back again,

'Oh no,' he said. 'There's two of you.'

Then he went upstairs and closed his bedroom door and we haven't heard a word from him since.

Like I said, lovely Josette.

SUNDAY 17TH JUNE

I took Josette to Megs's house to meet everybody. Not that Josette was particularly bothered by introductions; she just grabbed everyone and planted a smacky kiss on both cheeks. Including Westy and Elliot who were playing an army shooting game on Megs's computer.

'What is this game?' Josette asked. 'Can I play this? I am very good at ...' she mimed taking out a hoard of soldiers in a rain of machine gun fire, in a frighteningly realistic way.

Since Josette seemed to have made herself at

home, I pulled Megs into the hallway and asked, 'Where's Ethan?'

She looked at her shoes. 'He's not coming; he's seeing Dawn. I told Cam to tell him he could bring her, but . . .'

'But what?'

'He said that certain people have got a problem with her.'

'He means me, doesn't he?' This is unbelievable. This is what you get for trying to explain your passionate French fling to the boy you secretly want to date.

Megs put an arm around me. 'Listen, Faith, you can sort it out with him next time you see him. Don't let it spoil tonight.'

I sighed, but because I live for others I decided I shouldn't bring the party down, so I put on my best smile and headed for the pizza.

Later on, Westy challenged us all to an arm wrestling match.

'No thanks,' I said. 'I'm really fond of the way my arm is straight and moves smoothly and isn't full of shards of shattered bone.'

Westy pouted. 'No one ever wants to arm wrestle me.'

'That's because you've got twice as much arm as everybody else,' Megs said.

'I will wrestle you,' Josette said.

Westy looked startled. 'Really?'

'Yes, for real.'

Westy grinned and positioned his arm on the table.

Josette got up and went to sit down opposite him.

I had a bad feeling. 'Er, wait a minute, is this a good idea? Josette's mum is probably expecting her back with both arms.'

Josette looked between me and Westy. 'Actually,' she said. 'My mother, she will not be surprised if I break the arm. She said to me, do not break all the bones.'

'Oh well, as long as we keep the limbs in plaster down to a low number that's all right then,' I said.

Josette stretched out her arm, then placed her elbow on the table. She wiggled her fingers and clasped Westy's hand.

Westy's eyes widened. He was staring at their hands. I think touching Josette was an unexpected treat.

'Ready?' Josette asked.

Westy managed a nod.

'Go!'

Westy was still grinning at her.

Josette threw all her weight behind her arm. Westy's hand dropped a little towards the table.

'Westy!' Cam shouted. 'You're not going to let her beat you, are you?'

'What? Oh.' Westy pulled himself together and

pushed his arm back upright, but there it stopped. Josette scrunched up her face in effort, but she couldn't budge Westy and he was clearly enjoying holding Josette's hand too much to beat her and let it go.

We all watched Josette grimacing for several minutes.

Eventually, Westy made a big show of putting some effort into beating her.

'Next time I will win you!' Josette said panting.

'Yep, next time,' Westy said. And even though he can usually pin down anyone's arm without batting an eyelid, he was a bit flushed too.

MONDAY 18TH JUNE

School with Josette was great. The teachers are trying to be really serious with us because we've got mocks coming up, but Josette really cheered things up by asking a million questions. Mostly about what the teachers were wearing.

On the way home, Lily said, 'So, do you like Westy, Josette?'

'I like Westy very much. He is so ...'

'Big?' Angharad asked.

'Powerful. He could squash all the people, but no! He does not squash, he is too kind.'

'Sometimes he squashes people,' Megs said. 'Once he didn't notice Elliot tucked up under a cushion and he squashed him quite a lot, and there was that time he sat on my cheesecake – mind you, he ate it afterwards and didn't even leave a crumb. Anyway, those were accidents. He'd never use his strength for evil.'

Josette smiled. 'And he is funny; very funny. Yesterday when he is telling the story of his mother finding his head that is not the real head in her bed, I am laughing so much that I am – how do you say it?'

'Hiccupping?' Lily suggested.

Josette shook her head.

'Snorting?' I asked.

'No, like this.' And Josette mimed what was unmistakably a fart.

Lily laughed so hard that I was afraid she might let rip too. I took a step away from her.

'Hmm,' I said to Josette. 'You two do seem really suited. Do you think you might kiss him?'

Josette gave a firm nod. 'Yes, I will. Soon.'

I like a girl who knows her own mind.

I wish I had plans to kiss Ethan soon. But he still thinks I don't like his girlfriend. Which I don't, but since I'd tried so hard not to let him know that, it seems pretty unfair that that's what he's thinking.

TUESDAY 19TH JUNE

During registration Miss Ramsbottom called all the prefect applicants into the hall.

'As you know, prefect interviews begin in two weeks. Make sure you look at the schedule pinned up on the Year Ten noticeboard and make a note of the date and time of your interview. I trust you will all take this seriously and present yourself in the best possible light. It's an excellent opportunity to practice your interview skills for when you'll be applying for college and jobs.'

I rolled my eyes at Megs. Why are teachers so determined that school should be a time for practising for the real world? I know that when I'm a grown up I'm going to have to be sensible and polite and not express myself by throwing water bombs, so why can't I just take it easy while I'm at school?

This evening, I asked Josette if she thought I would make a good prefect.

'This prefect is telling all the girls what it is they must do?'

'Basically, yeah.'

'I think you will be *magnifique*.'

WEDNESDAY 20TH JUNE

Today was Angharad and Eliot's turn to debate. I was quite nervous for them, I knew that both of them would have written really good speeches, but I thought that we might all need those ear trumpets that elderly people had in the olden days when my dad was a boy, to hear them.

'How are you feeling about doing your debate?' I asked her at lunchtime.

'Pretty okay. Louise helped me practice last night, didn't you?'

Louise nodded.

It's interesting; since Louise has been here, Angharad has worked so hard at looking after her that she's actually been more chatty and confident.

When the boys arrived Ethan wasn't with them.

'He said he couldn't be bothered,' Cam said. 'But I think he might be in trouble with his parents. His mum rang him at lunchtime today and she didn't sound happy. I reckon she told him to come home straight after school.'

I felt a bit sorry for him then. Parents are such a pain, always wanting you to be somewhere or not somewhere. Maybe I should make an effort to sort things out with him. Even if he was a bit rude and jumpy-to-conclusiony. To be honest, I'm a bit nervous about speaking to him. Things between us seem so volatile.

I concentrated on Ang after that, but I needn't have worried about her. She made eye contact with the audience and used the loudest voice I've ever heard from her. Actually, she was still a weeny bit quiet, but that just meant that everyone in the room was completely silent so that we could all hear. Which is a pretty good technique really.

Miss Ramsbottom should try that one instead of bellowing at us all the time.

Ang and Elliot won easily and success seemed to have a powerful effect on Ang, because as we were walking home from Juicy Lucy's she suddenly announced, 'Elliot's going to be my boyfriend now.'

'Angharad!' I squealed.

Megs was thumping her on the back, Josette and Louise started singing in French and Lily danced with a lamppost (mind you, she's done that before even when a celebration wasn't in order.)

I pulled Ang round to face me. 'How did this happen? Did he ask you?'

'No. I asked him.'

'Wow!' said Megs. 'That was brave.'

Ang looked at me and I beamed back at her. She really has been amazing today.

Maybe I should try harder to confront the stuff that scares me.

LATER

Like speaking to Ethan.

THURSDAY 21ST JUNE

I told Dad that Josette and I had been invited round to Westy's house tomorrow night.

'Not another party. Don't you go to Westy's house rather a lot? How do his poor parents feel about this?'

'It's more of a gathering than a party. Anyway, it's fine; his house is massive and his parents are sensible types who know how important it is for teenagers to see a crowd of friends on a regular basis.'

'I see. Yes, I'm sure I'd be more liberal with you if we could keep five rooms between us.'

'His parents are also lovely people who care about his happiness.'

But this was lost on Dad because he'd started sketching on the back of an envelope. He was muttering something about adding a separate wing to the house.

FRIDAY 22ND JUNE

As soon as we arrived at Westy's, Josette marched right up to him and asked, 'Are you going to dance with me?'

Westy swallowed and nodded.

They were quite something. Westy seemed to be working his way through all the cheesy dance crazes of the last hundred years while Josette was a bit more freestyle. She twirled around Westy, and at one point used him as a sort of launching pad by clambering up him and throwing herself off his sturdy thigh. Overall, it was mesmerising.

When Ethan arrived I decided to follow Josette's go-getting example and I went straight up to him and said, 'Can I talk to you?'

He shrugged. 'All right.'

'About last week. You got the wrong end of the stick; I honestly wasn't talking about Dawn. I was talking about me, which shouldn't really come as a surprise because I am my favourite topic of conversation. I was thinking about my own relationships, and I mean they've been fun and all, but I was just reflecting that maybe next time I date someone, I might choose someone that I've really got something in common with.'

He gave me a long look. I couldn't tell if he thought I was making it all up or if he thought there was something odd about what I'd said.

'Okay,' he said. 'I probably shouldn't have over reacted. I just … I don't know. I've got a lot going on at the moment. I'm a bit uptight.'

At least he'd stopped scowling at me. 'Well, I always find Westy's gatherings super relaxing.'

We looked around at the utter madness going on in Westy's kitchen.

He grinned. 'Yep. Nice quiet evening at Westy's should sort me out.'

I pointed out Westy dancing with Josette. 'He looks like he's having a good time, doesn't he?'

'He does. It's touching to see two young people come together who share a love of expressing themselves through dance.'

'Yep. They're also perfectly suited in levels of utter craziness.'

'I think Josette might be the top scorer there, but they can certainly pursue their interest in demolishing other people's property together.'

At this point, Westy was accidentally trampling someone's bag and Megs was snatching away a lamp before Josette could crash into it.

I wondered what exactly Ethan meant when he said he had a lot going on. Had he rowed with Dawn? He didn't look upset; he looked gorgeous.

'What?' he asked.

I hadn't realised I was staring. Obviously, I couldn't tell him that I'd just been thinking about touching his cheek, so I said the first thing that came into my head. Unfortunately that was, 'Do you want to dance with me?'

He seemed startled by that. 'Er, remember how I once said that I'm only really interested in doing activities that I can shine at and make other people feel inferior with my skill, therefore boosting my own self esteem?'

'I'm not sure you ever said that.'

'But you knew it anyway?'

I laughed. 'So you're not big on dancing?'

'You know how all the little bees have different jobs? Some of them work, some of them look after the queen and some of them probably dance really well, in their bee-ish way. Well, I'm the bee that hangs about saying sarcastic things.'

'Yes you are.'

'So I'm more of a talker than a dancer. Do you want to talk with me?'

I really did.

We talked about Ang and Elliot getting together and about how childish parents can be. It was nice.

LATER

By the end of the evening Westy and Josette were looking very friendly. I won't go into details, but I'll just say that it turns out that Josette and Westy's snogging style is equally as energetic and crazy as their dancing.

SATURDAY 23RD JUNE

Since Josette's school arranged for us to go on a trip to Paris, you'd think my lot could have taken us to London. Nope.

I did suggest to Mum she might like to drive us there, but she packed us off to look at the cathedral. All I'm saying is you can take a look at a cathedral just as well from the outside as the inside.

Anyway, all Josette really wanted to do was snog Westy. I convinced Lily to come along and have a picnic, so that I had someone to talk to and something to snack on while I watched Westy and Josette chomping on each other. They did stop occasionally to tell rude jokes and tickle each other. At one point

Westy rolled over Josette and I feared she'd be crushed so flat that I'd have to airmail her back to France, but everything seemed to ping back into place.

'They're quite … athletic with their kissing, aren't they?' Lily said. 'Me and Arif usually don't jump up and down when we kiss.'

'Yeah, and I'm not sure anyone should try walking on a wall while snogging. That sort of thing ends up with broken teeth and someone's mum saying, "What were you thinking?"'

I managed to get her home all in one piece and we stayed up late chatting. Josette mostly talked about Westy and I may have mentioned Ethan's name once or twice.

SUNDAY 24TH JUNE

Westy came to see Josette off this morning. It was loud. Westy sang while Josette thumped on the coach window and started acting out some sort of story using other people's heads as puppets.

They seemed to enjoy themselves. I'm glad Westy has found someone, even though their love will now be tested by great distance. They've made tons of plans for the summer holidays and they're going to Skype a lot, and, as I said to Megs, it won't even matter if their computers break, the volume those two chat at, they'll still be able to hear each other across the Channel.

I was really sad to see that sweet mega mouth girl go.

LATER

After I'd seen Josette off I was drifting through town wondering if there would be anything decent for lunch, or if I should take the precaution of filling up on jelly babies, when something on the other side of the road, in the window of McDonald's, caught my eye. It was a purple hooded top with stars on like the one Dawn was wearing that time she and Ethan came round to Westy's. What really got my attention was the fact that the person in the hoodie was attached to the mouth of a tall blond boy. Dawn was kissing someone who definitely wasn't Ethan.

I stopped and stared.

Someone bumped into me from behind. 'Don't block up the pavement!' A man snapped at me.

I started walking again. Trying to get a better look at the purple hoody person in between the moving traffic, she'd turned her face away now, but I was sure it was Dawn.

Wasn't it?

I needed to get across the road, but the cars were streaming past. I sped down the street to the crossing on the corner. My heart was speeding. What was I doing? Was this spying on Dawn? I mean I can pop into Maccy D's if I want to. Besides, if you're going to snog in a window then you obviously don't care who sees you.

But by the time I'd crossed over, hurried back up the road and got inside McDonald's, the purple hoody and the blond boy were gone. I was sure they hadn't come past me so they must have gone out the side entrance.

I rang Megs.

She sucked in her breath when I told her. 'Was it definitely her?'

'Yes, I mean, I think so. I was sure it was her when I first saw them, but I never got to have a second look.'

'Poor Ethan,' Megs said. 'Are you going to tell him?'

'Of course.' I hesitated. 'Or maybe not. I'm not a hundred percent sure. What if it just starts a big argument between them and they end up splitting up, but all the time she was innocent?'

'That would be perfect, wouldn't it?'

'No! I want Ethan to choose to be with me, not to end up with me because I've sabotaged his relationship.'

'That's not what you're trying to do.'

'No, but it might *look* like that's what I'm trying to do. I've only just managed to convince him that I wasn't telling him to split up with her last week. If I tell him this, he'll just think that I'm bad mouthing her again.'

'Hmm.'

'I'm not sure that I should say anything. I don't think I should meddle.'

'But you love meddling!'

'I'm trying to give it up.'

'Maybe he's fine with it; maybe that's why he nearly snogged you at the carnival. Perhaps they've got that sort of relationship.'

'Doesn't sound very nice to me. But I suppose it is their relationship and we don't know anything about it. I'm just going to keep my mouth shut – unlike Dawn.'

MONDAY 25TH JUNE

I keep thinking about Dawn. Actually, it's Ethan I'm thinking about. I know that the whole thing is none of my business, but if one of my friends saw my boyfriend kissing someone who wasn't me, I'd want them to tell me.

LATER

Except, of course, I don't actually know how their boyfriend-girlfriend thing works. Maybe they've got some sort of arrangement like Megs said. Maybe if I tell Ethan I saw Dawn with another boy he'll laugh and say "So what?".'

LATER STILL

Even though it's none of my business and there's a teeny tiny possibility that it wasn't even Dawn, (just someone who looks exactly like her and has the same clothes as her) and even though Ethan will probably think I'm a jealous liar who is trying to interfere with his relationship, I think I am going to have to say something to him at debating club. At least then I'll have tried to do the right thing.

TUESDAY 26TH JUNE

At lunchtime Icky came prancing up to me and Angharad, like an evil My Little Pony.

'I saw you on Sunday afternoon,' she said to Ang. Which is one of those stupid statements that I think is best responded to with a kick in the head.

Angharad, of course, has neither my violent tendencies nor my powerful leg muscles so she just nodded.

'You were with that titchy Radcliffe boy. Is he your boyfriend? I bet people mistake him for your little brother, don't they?

Ang was turning pink. 'His name is Elliot an—'

'And it's none of your business who he is,' I said. 'We don't ask impolite questions about who you're hanging about with, Vicky. Mostly because it would take too long to learn to recognise all the different species of troll you're friends with.'

'Don't insult my friends!'

'All right, we can go back to insulting you if you like.'

'I'm not the weirdo that was on a date in a museum.' She turned back to Angharad. 'You're so sad.'

Angharad flinched.

'I think it's sadder that you had so little to do on your Sunday that you had to *watch* people on a date in a museum,' I said.

'I go on dates in the evening like a normal person.'

Angharad forehead crumpled into a frown. 'Yeah, well ... you wouldn't have enjoyed it in the museum anyway, you wouldn't have understood any of it.'

There was a burst of laughter and I realised the girls on the table behind us had been listening in.

'Good one, Angharad!' Becky said.

Icky opened her mouth to say something, but everyone was so pleased that lovely Ang had got one over on evil Icky that whatever nastiness came out of her big gob was completely lost in cheering and high fives.

WEDNESDAY 27TH JUNE

Angharad and I sat together this afternoon. It was Geography, so we were able to have a good chat because there wasn't much else going on.

'Do you think it's weird to go on a date to a museum?' she asked me.

'I would think it much weirder if you and Elliot had gone clubbing.'

'Why? People go clubbing with their boyfriends, don't they?'

I took my yoghurt out of my bag and pulled off the lid. 'I think the whole idea of a date is that you do something that you both enjoy. The museum is perfect for you and Elliot.'

'Perfect for geeks.'

'There's nothing wrong with being a geek. It's just a word that people use when they're jealous of how smart you are. It's people like you who end up with the best jobs and get the most out of life. Icky's too stupid to even enjoy a museum or an art gallery. We should feel sorry for her really.'

'I suppose so. It's just … I mean, I'm really glad Elliot likes the same stuff as me and I don't really care what Icky thinks is a good place for a date, but sometimes I wonder if we're doing other stuff right.'

'What other stuff?' I asked.

Her cheeks were flushed. 'Kissing stuff.'

'There isn't really a right or a wrong way as long as you're happy. Are you enjoying the kissing stuff?'

Angharad looked at the desk. 'There hasn't actually been any kissing stuff. I mean, Louise was here last week and then I saw him on Sunday after she'd gone and, well, nothing really happened.'

'Oh. That's okay. Do you want kissing to happen?'

'Maybe. We did hold hands for a bit in the Egyptian room at the museum. That was nice.'

The yoghurt hadn't filled much of a hole so I rummaged around in my lunch box again. 'Elliot obviously likes you a lot. I'm sure you'll get to the kissing. It's the same as the museum. You don't have to follow anybody else's idea of what's the right way to do it. Do what's best for you and Elliot.'

She nodded. 'That makes sense.' She grabbed her pen and bent over her work. 'Faith,' she whispered. 'Mr Cox is glaring at you.'

And then I had to listen to a long lecture about how we weren't in the cafeteria and I should be thinking about my work not eating my lunch. Fortunately, I still had half a Kit Kat in my mouth, so sucking on that helped pass the time.

LATER

Ethan turned up late to debating club. Mrs Lloyd-Winterson had already launched into her introduction so there was no chance to speak to him then. I kept trying to catch his eye during the debate, but he spent almost the whole time staring out the window. Maybe he was thinking about Dawn. He didn't look too happy though. When it was all over I shot out of my chair, but it's quite hard to clear a pack of teenagers to one side even when you do use my special chop-and-pinch technique. I called out,

'Ethan! Wait up!' but either he didn't hear me or he pretended not to. By the time I'd got down the stairs and outside he'd completely disappeared.

Why is doing the right thing so difficult?

And why does it have to involve running?

EVEN LATER

I was sort of relieved that I didn't have to try to find the words to tell him about Dawn. But I can't put it off forever, so I've sent him a text asking if he's coming to the park with everybody after school on Friday. I'll tell him about Dawn then.

THURSDAY 28TH JUNE

I'd just sauntered into school this morning and was wondering if Lily had arrived yet, (or more specifically if Lily's lunch had arrived) when I was startled by Miss Ramsbottom appearing out of nowhere.

I looked around for a secret door. There wasn't one, so I think that this confirms Miss R's vampire abilities once and for all.

She was eyeing me up and down like I imagine you do when you're deciding whether to buy a cow or not, so I said, 'Nothing to see here. Just hurrying to my education, Miss Ramsbottom, with barely any contraband in my bag.'

She ignored all that. 'Faith, could I have a moment of your time?'

That's the first time she's ever actually asked if I want to spend time with her. Normally she just starts bellowing at me without so much as a 'Did you see Eastenders last night?'. I was tempted to tell her that I didn't have a moment to spare because all my moments at school are taken up with snacking, flicking things at Megs and making up songs about Mr Hampton's moustache, but curiosity got the better of me, so I decided to see what she wanted.

'As you are aware,' she said looking down at me from her incredibly high-heeled heels. 'I have been organising the Green Schools Alliance conference, which is happening today.'

'Oh, yes. I noticed the date ringed on my calendar of exciting school events as I leapt out of bed to get in a bit of simultaneous equations practice this morning.'

She eyed me up and down like I imagine you do when the cow you are thinking about buying produces a cowpat on your foot. 'Yes, well, unfortunately, Sushma, who was due to give the main speech on our school's green initiative is unwell.'

I could see where this one was heading. 'That won't look good for you, will it?'

She bristled like a brand new toothbrush. 'Obviously, it's not really my fault, but I would like our visitors to hear about the good work the school is doing.'

I remembered how enthusiastic Ang has been about this whole Green thing. 'You could ask Angharad to do the speech.'

She shook her head. 'Angharad is already busy acting as a guide. And, although she has exceptional organisational skills and is a lovely girl, she is perhaps a little ...'

'Quiet?'

'... Shy.'

'So what you're looking for is someone who is loud and full of personality?'

'Yes, I suppose so.'

'That's funny because ordinarily I find myself getting told off for those qualities.'

'There's no need to be cheeky, Faith. I am asking you if you would be prepared to take on the speech.'

I pretended to consider it. Ramsbum clearly needed my help and I was determined to make the most of it. 'If I learnt this speech at the last minute and demonstrated admirable levels of eloquence and charisma then I'd really be a credit to the school, wouldn't I?'

I had the pleasure of watching a small part of her die inside while she nodded.

'The sort of girl that would be a real asset to the prefect team?'

The penny dropped. Her eyes hardened. 'Yes, Faith, if you deliver this speech with your usual aplomb I will definitely put in a good word about you to the prefect selection committee.'

I beamed. 'Obviously, I was always going to say yes.'

'Obviously.'

And she handed me the speech with what I thought was an unnecessarily frosty glare given that I had just volunteered to save her bony behind.

I sauntered off to registration.

'Are you eating custard creams again, Mrs Webber?' I asked, leafing through the speech. 'Because I may have to requisition them. I've got important work to do for the good of the school; I've got to learn this whole speech before eleven o'clock and I find I memorise better on a full stomach.'

'Nope,' said Mrs Webber through a suspiciously full mouth. 'No biscuits here. What's this speech?'

'Miss Ramsbottom has entrusted me with the extremely difficult task of making her look like a decent human being who doesn't hate students and totally cares about the environment.'

Mrs W raised her eyebrows.

'I know. It's a big ask, even for a girl of my talents. Basically, I've got to do this speech thing for those green people at the green thing. I'm the only person that can save her backsi— er, her back bacon.'

Mrs W brushed biscuit crumbs off her front. 'Is it that, or is it that she's desperate?'

I waved the three page speech at her. 'Can you

think of anyone else who could learn all this at the last minute?'

'I'm not sure that *you* can learn it at the last minute.'

I looked down at the speech, there was rather a lot of it. 'Maybe not, but I will carry off having not learnt it with style. Come on, wouldn't you turn to me in an emergency?'

Mrs W gave it some thought. 'No.'

I was a bit disappointed by this. 'But I've got a lot of transferable skills! I'm strong and smart ...'

'Violent and volatile,' Mrs W added. 'Listen, I tell you what, if I'm ever murdered under suspicious circumstances I give you my full permission to avenge my death.'

'I'd be honoured. And should the zombie apocalypse happen before you get truly ancient – let's say thirty-eight, shall we? Then you're very welcome to join my army.'

'Sounds delightful. Now, hadn't you better sit down and get on with half-learning that speech?' And she swivelled round on her spinning chair so she had her back to me and carried on eating custard creams.

By selflessly working on it all through double RE I knew that speech inside out by eleven o'clock. I'd even added a few touches of my own. I was a teeny bit nervous before I had to stand up in front of dozens of teachers from other schools, but I managed to get through the whole thing and they seemed to like it. Miss Ramsbottom was clearly ecstatic. I could tell this because when I finished she threw caution to the wind and forgot about her brittle bones and clapped her hands together. Twice. That's how good I was.

LATER
I've got to say the knowledge that Miss Ramsbottom owes me a favour is making me quite dizzy with joy.

FRIDAY 29TH JUN
I was planning my speech to Ethan all the way to the park but as soon as I got there and saw Megs's face I knew something was up.

'What?' I asked.

Her face clouded. 'He's not coming. Cam says he's split up with Dawn.'

'No!'

'Yep, and you'll never guess why.'

My head was spinning. 'Why?'

'Apparently someone told him that they saw Dawn kissing someone else.'

I let out a breath. 'So it *was* her. Is he upset?'

'I don't know. He didn't say much to Cam, just that he'd broken it off with Dawn and he didn't fancy coming out.' She was watching me.

'What?' I asked.

'Well, he's single now, isn't he?'

I bashed her over the head.

But I won't say that it hadn't occurred to me.

In fact, all the time we were sat on the swings, (watching Westy attempt to make Elliot fly off the roundabout, by spinning it at the speed of light and then stopping it dead) Ethan and his singleness kept pinging into my head. But there's no reason to think that just because he's split with up with Spawn that he'll be interested in me.

SATURDAY 30TH JUNE

Since everyone has been going on and on about the mock exams, and since I really quite like not failing stuff, I decided to spend today revising. It started out quite dull but then I got inventive and started making up songs to help me remember stuff and acting out history with Sam's teddies. I think I've covered a lot of ground.

They should put me on kids' TV.

By the evening I was more than ready for a bit of relaxation.

I said to Dad, 'I'm going to meet the others by the river.'

Dad nodded in a way that clearly suggested that he didn't think that I'd done enough revision.

'I've been revising all day.'

He nodded again.

'There's only so much you can do in one session. You don't want me to become so loaded with knowledge that my little brain explodes, do you?'

'That would certainly be bad news for the curtains. I've only just got out that mustard stain your grandmother left. I wish she'd just use a napkin like everybody else.'

'So ... I'm going.'

'Make sure you're back before dark. Have a nice time.'

I sighed heavily. 'I'll try. At least it will be a break from your constant nagging.'

I picked up Megs and a jumbo tube of Smarties and we went to meet the others.

'Warm isn't it?' Megs said. 'Perfect night for getting romantic. Do you think Ethan will be there?'

I gave her a look. 'If he is, he's not going to be in the mood for romance, is he? He's just split up with his girlfriend.'

'So? Out with the old and in with the new.'

Oh my. I had to put a stop to this before she really got started. 'Promise you won't say anything stupid to Ethan?'

'Of course not.' And she mimed locking up her lips, which was a waste of time because she had to unlock them to carry on shovelling in Smarties at a rate that meant I barely managed to eat more than a few dozen myself.

As soon as we caught sight of the others sat under a tree, Megs shouted, 'Ethan! Faith's here!'

If I'd thought I could have spat a mouthful of Smarties at her while still looking attractive I would have done it.

LATER

It was a while before Ethan and I ended up sat next to each other.

'Sooooo,' I said in an attempt to fill up the silence.

'So, I split up with Dawn?'

'I wasn't going to say anything about that. Honestly.'

'That would have been weird.' He pushed his hair out of eyes. 'Look, it's all right, Faith. I'm fine. I mean, quite hacked off and feeling a bit depressed-annoyed-hungry, but generally fine.'

I handed him the tube of Smarties.

'Thanks.'

'I'm sorry,' I said. 'Breaking up sucks.'

'It's all right. I think it was for the best. I mean, I am a little put out that someone would rate a big-jawed athletic type over me and my skinny-but-interesting look, but the point is, I think Dawn and I have got very different ideas about going out with someone. If I like someone then I'm *with* them, but Dawn was more into ...'

'Getting friendly with someone else over a Big Mac?'

His expression changed.

'Big Mac?'

Uh oh.

'I thought … didn't she snog the big-jawed athlete in McDonalds?'

'Where did you hear that?' The intensity of his voice made me really wish I'd kept my mouth shut.

'Because it wasn't from me,' he snapped. 'I never heard anything about McDonalds. Ryan told me that he'd seen her at the skate park with some idiot.'

'Oh.' Why did I open my big mouth? And why did he still care how many sporty types Spawn had kissed?

'So what's this about the McDonalds?'

'It's nothing. It doesn't matter.'

'Where did you hear it?' He was staring at me hard; clearly he wasn't going to let this drop.

'If you really want to know, since you seem to care so much, even though you said you were fine about breaking up; I saw her kissing a boy,' I said. 'At least, I think I did.'

His face clouded. 'And you didn't say anything?'

'I wasn't sure! And I didn't think it was any of my business and then I *was* going t—'

'You should have told me!' He said it so loudly

that everyone else stopped talking and turned around to look at us.

A minute ago we were having a nice chat and now he was angry with me because Dawn had messed him about.

'I can't believe you, Faith!'

'Hey! It's not my fault that your ex-girlfriend is a serial snogger.'

I expected him to keep right on shouting, in fact, I wish he had. Instead he said in this bitter voice, 'You know what, Faith? I've had enough of fighting and I've had enough of people being idiots.'

And he walked off.

Which put a bit of a dampener on the happy atmosphere.

I felt horrible. The others all agreed that it wasn't my fault that Spawn had upset him, but I know that that's not really the point. He was disappointed in me; I could see it in his eyes.

I should have told him.

JULY

SUNDAY 1ST JULY

I'm so miserable about Ethan that it's actually been a relief to throw myself into revision and rehearsing what I'm going to say to the prefect selection committee.

LATER

All the little molecules in my Chemistry book kept rearranging themselves into Ethan's face, so in the end I called him. He didn't answer. On the fifth attempt I left a rambling message about how sorry I am for not telling him about Dawn. I hope he listens to it.

MONDAY 2ND JULY

All the teachers are talking about at school is how the mocks are next week. They keep telling us how hard we all need to study. I wish they'd stop lecturing and maybe give us some hints on what exactly we need to revise. Every time I asked Mrs McCready if something was going to be on the exam paper she said, 'It could be, Faith.'

'This is ridiculous. You're basically saying that anything we've learnt in the last year could be in the exam.'

'That's right.'

'So you're expecting us to remember everything that we've been taught?'

She nodded.

Seriously, that would be difficult enough if I had been listening the first time she taught it to us, but as it is I've got to learn the entire syllabus in a week.

Teachers have very unrealistic expectations of what teenagers can fit in around the bare minimum of eating, sleeping, texting and TV watching.

And moping about stupid boys.

LATER

I asked the girls if they were ready for the prefect interviews this week. Angharad has rehearsed her response to fifty-seven possible questions. Megs says she's thought about it and Lily seems to think that whatever comes out of her mouth at the time will be fine.

Given that, on various occasions, I've seen pebbles, elastic bands and a life size model of a gerbil come of Lily's mouth, I'm not so sure.

TUESDAY 3RD JULY

I'm having a bad day. I haven't heard from Ethan and there's no way I can revise everything that I need to know before next week.

I'd been working solidly all evening, but then I started thinking about the prefect interviews on Thursday. I'd just started making notes about what someone who was definitely a prefect type might say when Mum came in and said, 'Is that revision?'

'No, it's not revision! It's for the prefect interview. I keep telling you, I can't revise every single minute!'

Mum sat down on my bed and put a hand on my shoulder. 'Is everything all right, sweetheart?'

'No it's not! My main problem is that I am trying to write something really intelligent and you're clouding the water by saying stupid stuff.' Then I felt bad because she was obviously trying to be nice. 'I've just got so much to do.'

She slipped an arm around me. 'Do you think it might be time to take a break? You barely even stopped for your tea.'

'I don't need a break. I need to think of some convincing lies that will persuade a bunch of doddering idiots that I am very sweet and honest and an obvious choice as a prefect.'

'You're taking this prefect business very seriously.'

She was laughing at me. 'I do take things seriously sometimes, you know. It's nice that people have got this image of me as being all super happy and light all the time, but I am quite capable of being serious too.'

'I know you are. I'm your Mum. I remember that project on Egyptians at primary school when you built a papier mache pyramid, complete with the burial chamber inside. And I remember the night before your first ever exam. I know you don't like it to get out, but I do know how hard you work on things that are important to you.'

'Keep that to yourself, will you? We'll let the rest of the world think I'm naturally brilliant.'

'You are naturally brilliant, love, and when you want to be, you're also a good worker. I'm very proud of you for that, but I don't like to see you getting upset and I'm wondering why this prefect interview is so important, because keeping the rules and supporting the teachers has never been one of your special interests before.'

I took a deep breath and for some stupid reason a little tear leaked out of the corner of my eye.

'I just wanted to do a good interview,' I sniffed. 'Everything has gone wrong recently. I keep messing things up: I upset Megs over that French exchange business, now I've upset Ethan, even though I honestly did try to tell him his girlfriend was cheating. And I've got so much work to do before the exams. I thought this would be something I could do; everybody else seems to think I can ace it so I just . . .' Two more tears leaked out.

Mum hugged me. 'I'm sorry you're having a tough time, darling. Friends have their ups and downs. Everything is fine with Megs now, isn't it?'

I nodded.

'Megan loves you. I can tell that all your friends think you're great. I'm sorry if Ethan is cross, maybe you can talk to him about it?'

'Maybe.'

'As for the exams, just do your best. It won't be the end of world if you fail them.'

'I'm not going to fail them! I never said anything about failing them!'

Mum laughed. 'Then try not to get too stressed; it doesn't matter if you're not top of the class.'

Obviously it does matter, and I don't think I'm going to be able to avoid getting stressed, but it was still nice to hear her say that.

There was some more hugging.

'Now, about this prefect interview. This is voluntary, isn't it? Are you sure you really want to do it?'

I thought about it. 'I do. I think it will be fun. You get to be in charge of stuff and I am good at organising things.'

'You mean you're bossy?'

'Yes.'

'Okay, but I don't want you to tie yourself up in knots about this interview. I have to say that I've always found you're ready with a smart answer even without rehearsals.'

That's true.

'So maybe you should just take the interview as

it comes, be your usual energetic, persuasive self and if that's not what they're looking for, stuff 'em.'

Which is quite good advice when you think about it.

LATER

I feel a lot better. I'm pretty sure I can convince some old people that I'm not as bad as I look. After all, I do it with Granny all the time. Exam-wise, I just have to make sure I revise every day. I already know more now than I did a week ago, so I've made a good start.

And as for Ethan, I've decided that I want him to know that I did try to tell him about Spawn, but ultimately if he's going to hold a mistake against me and stop liking me because I'm not perfect, then that's his loss.

WEDNESDAY 4TH JULY

I was so determined to speak to Ethan that I met the boys arriving for debating club at the gates.

'Ethan? Can I speak to you?' I asked.

'You can,' he said, without looking at me properly. 'But whether you do seems to depend on if you've got something that you really ought to tell me. Because I find if you have then you usually don't speak.'

I wasn't going to let his sarcasm get to me. 'It's

hardly fair to say "usually". I've only failed to tell that your girlfriend is snogging someone else once.'

'As far as I know.'

'It was only once, I promise.'

'It doesn't matter.' He carried on striding across the car park.

'It does matter,' I said, trying to match his pace. 'I feel terrible that I didn't tell you. The thing is that, apparently, I've got quite a big mouth and for once in my life I didn't want to just blurt out something if it was the wrong thing to do.'

He pushed open the door to the English block and turned back to look at me. 'How could it be the wrong thing to do?'

All the reasons that I had originally come up with disappeared from my mind. 'Believe it or not, I did actually decide to tell you, but you rushed off after debating club last week, so I thought I'd tell you on Friday, at the park, but you didn't turn up then either.'

He took the stairs two at a time. 'And your texting thumbs were in plaster?'

'That didn't seem like a particularly sensitive way to break the news.'

'For future reference, if you think that someone is cheating on me, you can definitely let me know by text. Or telegram. Or a badger who enjoys running errands. Just so long as you tell me.'

'I will, I promise I will.'

'Yeah, well, you probably won't get the opportunity. I'm off relationships, they all seem to end badly.'

'Not always.'

He shrugged. There was a pause. We were stood in the doorway of Mrs Lloyd-Winterson's classroom by this point and I wondered if I should just leave it, but then he gave this big sigh.

'Listen Faith, I didn't mean to have a tantrum the other night.' He pushed his curls off his face and he looked so miserable that my heart hurt. 'I'm sorry for being horrible,' he said. 'I shouldn't take things out on you.'

'That's okay.'

His mouth did something that was almost a smile, but sadder and bitterer, then he dropped into a chair next to Cameron. His face was pale and there were rings around his eyes. I wanted to give him a hug, but I don't think our reconciliation has got that far yet.

I hope he's all right.

THURSDAY 5TH JULY

Prefect interviews tomorrow.

Still, it's really just half an hour of talking about myself.

I do that most Geography lessons.

FRIDAY 6TH JULY

I was worried about who would be on the panel for my interview. I was just praying that it wouldn't be Miss Ramsbottom.

Or any of the other teachers that I've tormented and harassed.

Which doesn't leave that many.

Fortunately, when I walked into the interview room, the three people I found were Miss Linnie, the new Art teacher who I've never even spoken to, Mrs Lloyd-Winterson and a woman I didn't recognise.

'Good afternoon, Faith,' the unknown lady said. 'I am chairperson of the school governors.' She looked like a Granny in an advert for sweets, with grey hair and a floral dress. I bet she's never worn a grass skirt.

'Good afternoon,' I said as if I completely meant it.

'We're going to ask you a few questions. If there's anything you can't answer just say so.'

She smiled and I smiled back. I don't think there's ever been any question that I didn't have an answer for.

I sat down and they all picked up their pens. Governor Lady cleared her throat. 'What qualities do you think a prefect needs, Faith?'

I'd thought about this one. 'I think a prefect needs to be an excellent communicator. Part of the prefects' role is representing the student body to the Leadership team. Obviously, you need to have a clear understanding of the needs of other students and you need to be able to communicate them. Prefects also represent the school in other areas, like the City Youth Council and I think confident, clear communication is important to enable them to represent the school in its best light.'

They nodded their heads and scribbled some things down, which I took as a good sign. Of course, they could have been writing *Has the eyes of a serial killer who hides bodies down wells* but I'm trying to stay positive.

'What experiences have you had that you think will help to make you a good prefect?' Miss Linnie asked.

Given that prefects are mostly used for herding unruly Year Seven and Eights I think that time I couldn't find the remote and was forced to watch a programme about how lions manage to position gazelles right where they can sink their teeth into them is probably the most relevant experience I've had, but instead I said, 'I think every day at Westfield high has helped to prepare me for being a prefect. The school has taught me to use my initiative; to recognise the needs of others; and, most of all, what a difference it makes when people work together.'

I thought I might have gone a bit far there on the sick-making scale, but they were all beaming like headlights so I pressed on. 'I've been a keen member of the choir, which has taught me about commitment. I've arranged a Christmas box delivery for the local elderly which was a great opportunity to hone my organisational skills, and I've also set up a debating club which has been a brilliant opportunity for us all to improve our speaking skills.'

'I can vouch for Faith's commitment to the debating club,' Mrs Lloyd Winterson said.

'You're certainly very eloquent,' Governor Lady said.

I nearly said, you should see me when I'm talking my Dad into giving me the last piece of cheesecake, but I got a hold of myself and smiled instead.

'If you were to become a perfect,' Mrs L-W said, 'what changes would you like to make at Westfield High?'

I controlled the urge to let the power go to my head and instantly dismiss Miss Ramsbottom.

'I'd like to build on the partnership that exists between the prefects and the teachers, perhaps by increasing the role of the student council. I think it's important that students feel they have a say in the running of their school.'

Governor Lady put down her pen. 'Now Faith, we've heard a lot about your leadership skills and your influence with your peers, so we would like to ask if you are interested in being considered for the position of head girl?'

I was a little bit surprised by this question. Obviously, I'm a natural choice to run this school. But up until this point it had seemed like maybe the school hadn't noticed my talents. In fact, Miss Ramsbottom is always putting me into detention for my impressive leadership skills, or what she calls 'being a bad influence.' Still, Miss Ramsbottom wasn't there and I could see that if I used my best persuasive powers, I was in with a good shot at being head girl. I opened my mouth to share my marvellousness with them, but for once in my life that's not what came out.

Instead, I said, 'I don't think I'm the best girl for the role.'

They exchanged nervous glances.

'But I'll tell you who is: Angharad Jones would make an excellent head girl. Angharad is the one who first got me interested in applying to be a prefect and her commitment to the school really is inspirational. I've talked about debating club, choir, and the Christmas boxes for the elderly; Angharad has been fully immersed in those projects and she also took a lead role in the Green Schools conference. She's also captain of the netball team and a student mentor.'

Miss Linnie and Mrs L-W exchanged glances. Governor Lady frowned a little. 'Well, thank you for the recommendation, Faith, but I'm sure Angharad can tell us about her achievements.'

'But that's just it! She won't, she's too modest. She won't tell you that she's likely to get the highest marks in the mocks, or that, unlike most of the girls you see today who have both friends and enemies, Angharad is universally well liked and respected. And that includes the younger girls because she takes an interest in them and gives up her time to help tutor the ones who are struggling in maths.'

'I see.' Governor Lady made some notes. 'It certainly has been very interesting to hear this. Thank you, Faith, it's been a real pleasure meeting you.'

I'm not sure that you're supposed to start promoting other candidates when you're in an interview, but I have always been quite good at telling people what to do.

Anyway, Angharad has always supported me and it's obvious that she'd be a great head girl.

SATURDAY 7TH JULY

This morning I tried not to think about Ethan. I would have preferred to distract myself by wearing a prom dress and a million pounds worth of jewellery, while attending a film premiere, but instead I was stuck with memorising the carbon cycle. This afternoon I revised with the girls at Ang's house. I got more done by myself but it was more fun and more chocolatey with the others.

SUNDAY 8TH JULY

Mocks start tomorrow.

I don't know who first thought up mock exams. I'm pretty sure that Miss Ramsbottom had something to do with it.

We all know that GCSEs are big scary exams that affect your whole future and just to make sure you don't forget this, you get to sit in the tense, silent hall with teachers scowling to remind you how serious and important it all is. Who thought that recreating that scenario a whole year before the real thing was a good idea? Basically, we're practising for being stressed out and terrified by being stressed out and terrified.

Great.

I'm stressed out and terrified.

MONDAY 9TH JULY

Biology exam this morning. At lunchtime we collapsed in a heap.

'I don't think my brain is designed for memorising the structure of a cell and all that sort of thing,' Lily said.

I knew I shouldn't, but I couldn't help myself from asking, 'What is your brain designed for?'

She screwed up her face in concentration. 'It sort of sends me pictures.'

'Pictures?'

'Yeah, like what I'm going to have for lunch, or how cool my new socks would look with green baseball boots.'

'So you're saying you've got a mind for leisure rather than the book stuff?' I asked.

'Haven't we all,' Megs said.

'I'm pretty sure Angharad thinks in numbers,' I said, pointing at Ang who was measuring the angles of her Dorito with a protractor.

'That's not any weirder than thinking in socks and sandwiches,' Megs said.

Lily rubbed her temples with her fingers. 'You're good at revising, Faith. How do you get your brain to work?'

Angharad looked up to hear my answer.

I wriggled to get comfy. 'Are you sure you're ready for a scientific explanation? Because, after this morning, I am expecting an 'A' star in biology.'

Megs poked me in the ribs. 'Just tell us.'

'So … the way I see it, the brain is this amazing piece of equipment with the capacity to take in, er, stuff and to send it out again. Essentially, it's a sausage machine. If you just keep cramming it with meaty information, when you get to the exam you'll be able to crank out a long string of prime answer-sausages.'

Megs gave me a long look. 'I've just wasted a minute listening to that. I could have learnt something in that time.'

Angharad had already gone back to calculating the square on her Doritos' hypotenuse, but Lily was staring at me open-mouthed. 'Wow,' she said slowly. 'Now I get it.'

And she looked genuinely enlightened.

I couldn't help feeling quite pleased. 'Maybe I should be an educator,' I said.

Megs groaned. 'No way, it's bad enough having one of you. If they let you get your hands on impressionable young minds you'd only fashion yourself an army in your own image.'

'What's not to like about that?'

Megs walloped me with her bag.

Lily had opened her History textbook and was muttering 'Sausage machine, sausage machine.'

It's going to be a long week.

TUESDAY 10TH JULY

Exams. Revolting.

WEDNESDAY 11TH JULY

More exams. The highlight of the day was Icky falling off her chair during the maths paper. She pretended she'd fainted, but it was interesting how she managed to time it so that she fell at the feet of that fit student teacher. He looked horrified. Obviously, Icky couldn't see this because she had her eyes closed.

So after the exam I told her.

Several times.

THURSDAY 12TH JULY

During the French exam Miss Ramsbottom stood on the balcony and watched us. For an hour and a half. Without moving. She was definitely up to something. My bet is that she was using her vampire powers to drain us of our energy while our defences were down.

No wonder I'm exhausted.

FRIDAY 13TH JULY

After a miserable week of exams we agreed we should have a break and meet in the park tonight. When Megs and I got there, Ethan was sat on a bench staring into space looking both super-hot and a bit miserable. Westy and Lily were pretending to be horses, with Elliot and Angharad as their jockeys and Cameron was bellowing at them to go faster. I think the exam stress is getting to everyone.

Still, there's nothing wrong with letting off

steam so I placed a bet on Lily and Ang winning the obstacle race (it's probably a good thing they don't make real horses get on see-saws) and I won a Mars Bar off Cameron.

There was a lot of micky taking and laughing and a bit more pretending to be animals, so obviously I was having a pretty good time, but I thought Ethan still seemed a bit offish with me. He'd hardly said anything sarcastic to me all night.

Then I remembered that thing that Megs is always saying about how the world doesn't revolve around me, so I came at it from a new angle. And once my big head had deflated I thought that maybe there was something bothering him. Something non-me. So I went and sat on the swing next to him and said, 'How are you?'

'Fine.'

'You seem a bit down.'

'Oh, you know, the oppressive nature of the universe, global warming, Westy's run out of Jaffa Cakes. It's all weighing on me a bit heavily.'

'Is that it?'

'Also, I'm a surly teen. I don't go in for cheerful much.'

I didn't want to push it, but I didn't want to give up so I said, 'I'm a surly teen too, doesn't that mean that we cancel each other out like two negative numbers?'

He half smiled.

'I'm just trying to say that you don't have to be hilarious every minute that I'm talking to you.'

'So that means that up until this point in our friendship you consider everything I've said to be hilarious? Well, that's cheered me up considerably.'

I put my hand on his arm. 'Why do you need cheering up?'

He didn't say anything for several seconds.

'My parents are getting divorced.'

And suddenly a lot of stuff made sense. His moodiness, the aversion to arguments, what Cam had said about him having a bad time at home.

'Oh. That's rough. I'm really sorry.'

'Yeah, I mean, I'm not an idiot, despite what my form tutor says. It's not like I hadn't noticed that they weren't getting on brilliantly.' He picked at a thread on his jeans. 'I didn't expect us all to live happily ever after, it's just ...'

'You kind of wanted to?'

He nodded.

I thought really hard about what to say next.

'I can't pretend to know what you're going through and I don't want to say anything stupid like "you'll get used to it", but I feel bad for you, I really do.'

He bit his lip.

'Sorry, that's not much help is it?'

'It sort of is.'

'You know Lily's parents split up last year? Maybe you could talk to her.'

'I like talking to you. Unless you'd rather I shut up?'

'No. I like listening to you. You can talk as much as you like.'

And he did. He told me a lot of stuff about how horrible the last few months have been. How he's had to listen to his parents bickering all the time and how his dad has started trying to get him to take sides and how he wished he had a brother or sister because at least they'd understand.

It was the most serious conversation I'd ever had with him, but it was a really good one.

When we were walking home Megs said, 'That was an intense chat you were having with Ethan. You two didn't even stop to join in with the horsie hurdles, which Angharad won by the way; I had no idea she could jump that high. It would have been Lily but she couldn't stop laughing because Westy managed to get his trousers caught on the first hurdle and showed us all his Bugs Bunny boxers.'

'I didn't even notice.'

'I was sure you two were going to snog.'

Actually, I hadn't even thought about kissing Ethan. Well, maybe just a tiny bit when he said goodbye and squeezed my hand and I didn't want to let him go. Anyway, the rest of the time I was just thinking about Ethan.

There are more important things than kissing. Not many, but there are some.

SATURDAY 14TH JULY

Revision. I keep checking my ears to make sure my brain isn't dribbling out through them.

LATER

Ethan sent me a text. It said, *Thanks for cheering me up*.

It made me feel quite cheerful myself.

SUNDAY 15TH JULY

Today Mum made me some revision brownies. I let her into my room because she brought a delicious chocolatey smell with her.

She smiled at me. 'These should keep you going over the next couple of days.'

I'd already eaten two in the time it took her to put the plate down and say this.

'Well,' I said, spraying her with crumbs. 'They might keep me going over the next half hour anyway.'

'You're doing really well,' she said. 'Your dad and I are very proud of how hard you're working.'

I wished she hadn't said that, because now there was no avoiding the fact that my parents haven't actually been all that horribly annoying in the last week. In fact, a couple of times I've suspected them of being supportive.

I took a deep breath. 'Thanks. That's nice. Actually, I've got something to say to you. I've thought about it a lot so hear me out.'

Mum sat down.

I took a deep breath. 'So about this baby business: I'd just like to say that despite your advanced years and tendency to get a bit screechy when the smallest little heirloom gets broken, you are actually a fairly adequate parent. I mean, obviously you'll be too old to run around with the little one, but believe me children get more than enough sport rammed down their throats at school. You'll probably embarrass it with your dreadful clothes and your outdated views, but you were doing that to me even when you were in your twenties. Also you and Dad seem to have a really ... sturdy marriage and while I'm still banning you from expressing your affection in front of me, in any form other than a firm handshake, I do appreciate that you and Dad are, you know, together and stable. So all in all, I'm saying that if we ignore Sam, you have been pretty good parents and any baby would be lucky to have you. And I would help look after the baby as long as it wasn't early in the morning. Or late at night. Or when I'm watching something good on TV. But if you ever need me to miss school to play with it that's fine.'

There was a strange look on her face. I couldn't tell if she was going to cry or burst out laughing. She did a little gulpy thing. 'Oh Faith, I can't tell you how lovely that is to hear.'

'That's all right, you old prune.'

'The thing is that while you've just reminded me exactly why having children is so lovely, I don't think that we'll be adding to our household.'

Good grief. You would have thought that she could have let me know that before I felt moved to be nice.

'Why not?'

'I didn't realise that you'd given it so much thought. I wasn't really that serious when I said it. Most mothers when they hold a new-born feel a bit broody and start thinking about how wonderful babies are. But I realised afterwards that I wasn't thinking so much about a new baby and more about you and Sam when you were tiny. You were amazing. And you still are. I think our family is marvellous as it is, don't you?'

I popped another brownie in. 'Yeah, you're not bad.'

And then I let her hug me.

MONDAY 16TH JULY

History exam this morning. I've never written so much in my life. Towards the end I was going so fast that I didn't even have time to take the pen off the paper between words so my answer was just one big long series of loops.

I pity the person who has to mark that.

Surely they can just tell by how spidery my handwriting is that I'm an 'A' star student?

TUESDAY 17TH JULY

I feel like everything I have ever known has been scooped out of my head with a melon baller.

WEDNESDAY 18TH JULY

There was no debating club today because of the exams. It's crazy; I half expected McDonald's to have a sign up saying 'Closed due to exams' but fortunately the world outside Miss Ramsbottom's warped mind doesn't think that everything revolves around the exam hall.

We just popped into McD's to say hello to the boys. They've got their mocks too and obviously they wanted their morale boosting by some stimulating chat with us. Actually, Cam just slumped into Megs's arms muttering about their maths exam while she patted him on the head, but that seemed to cheer him up as well. We've all agreed that we're going to the 'Festival on the Farm' on Saturday to celebrate the end of term. The bands are mostly old hippies, but just the idea of being outside in the sun seems really appealing at the moment. In fact the idea of being anywhere where I don't have to remember loads of facts seems like heaven.

'How are the exams going?' I asked Ethan.

'You know me, I prefer it when people recognise my genius just by looking at me. If they really need convincing then I'm happy to say something bitingly witty, but being required to put things down on paper and back up my arguments by using facts, seems as if people are doubting my brilliance. Also, I'm quite lazy, but not quite enough to not care what marks I get. Which means ...' He leant in close and lowered his voice. '... I've actually had to do some work. Don't tell anyone or my reputation will be in shreds. Overall, the whole thing is making me quite irritable. You?'

'Pretty much the same.'

He smiled. He looked tired and I had this sudden urge to put an arm around him. Everything with his parents must be making all this exam stress ten times worse.

'And how's ... you know, things with your mum and dad?' I asked.

He twisted his mouth. 'Oh yeah, great. I'm thinking about breaking into song any minute.'

'I can keep a secret remember?'

He looked at his hands for a second. 'I guess I'm all right. Dad left on Sunday. That was pretty bad, but it is a relief not to listen to them yelling all the time.'

We had a good chat. Not just about his parents but about exams and pressure at school and the problem with everyone thinking you're a smart arse.

I even got to give him that hug at the end.

LATER

One more exam tomorrow. And then I am never thinking a single thing again.

THURSDAY 19TH JULY

Finished! I said to Mum and Dad this evening, 'I think we can all agree that I've given this school business a fair try. I've been at it for ten years and other than a few near exclusions, which I still consider to be down to nothing more than high spirits, I've done pretty well at it. But I've been thinking and I thought I'd let you know that I don't think it's for me. Exams are really quite tiring so I've decided not to bother with any more.' I smiled at them to show I was willing to make reasonable compromises. 'If you like I could wait till Christmas to drop out officially, as long as no one expects me to do PE or Geography during that time.'

Mum and Dad exchanged a look. 'You wouldn't want to leave school,' Mum said. 'What could you do without any qualifications?'

'You're always telling me that I can do anything I set my mind to.'

Dad shook his head. 'That's just something we say to encourage you. Obviously you can't do anything without good grades.'

'Listen, my kind of genius isn't the kind that you can measure.' I turned on Mum, 'I thought you believed that life is the greatest education anyway?'

'I do, but I'm not sure that many scientists agree with me. I thought you wanted to be a chemist?'

'A Nobel-prize winning chemist,' I corrected her. 'And I'm pretty sure that any employer would make an exception for me.'

'If you like you can take the whole summer off,' Dad said.

'Everyone is having the summer off.'

'We're not,' Mum said.

'You can if you want to; I give you permission. Just make sure we've got plenty of cash for meals out and holidays and things.'

'Faith, we know you've worked hard. Why don't you just forget about education for a bit and then in September we'll resume our nagging and you can get back to moaning.'

'I suppose so.'

And then Dad said, 'You've done really well with your revision.' And handed me several ten pound notes.

I blinked. 'Thank you, Father.' I gave them a gracious nod. 'Just so you know, next year when I do my real GCSEs, I'll be expecting diamonds.'

FRIDAY 20TH JULY

We've finally reached the end of term. I don't know why we've bothered with this last day. Everyone was exhausted from the mocks; I spent most of the morning snoozing. Megs said that the teachers just gave out word searches to those who'd remained conscious and then started looking for last minute holiday deals on line. When Megs woke me up to go to lunch I told Mrs McCready that she should forget about Portugal. If she really is as committed to the education of children as she claims to be, she ought to spend the holidays cleaning out the fish tank so I can concentrate on my Biology lessons instead of worrying about what those little eggs in the layer of green slime are going to hatch into. Mrs Mac said she needed a rest and I laughed. What does she think she's been doing all term? All I've witnessed while we swot away is her sitting at her desk eating Minstrels when she thinks we're not looking. She said a classroom full of teenagers was pretty tiring in itself. Honestly, why are old people so limp and lazy?

In the afternoon we had an end of term assembly where people get certificates for best kept socks and most sucking up to Ramsbottom and that kind of thing. I regretted sleeping through RE and biology because now I was wide awake and forced to listen to Miss R going on about how exciting it is that some Year Sevens went somewhere and did something and then drew some pictures about it. Maybe I'll just go back into Year Seven in September. Those sort of light colouring-in duties are about as much as I want to commit to.

I'd just managed to block out Miss R's droning by wrapping Ang's jumper around my head when Megs started poking me. It was time for the new prefects to be announced.

That woke me up. I thought about what Mum said, about it not being the end of the world if they didn't pick me. I could feel Icky's beady eyes on me. I knew if she was chosen and I wasn't, I'd never hear the end of it.

Miss R read out the list by tutor group. My old tutor group, Mrs Hatfield's, was first. I clutched Megs's hand.

'Megan Baptiste,' Miss R said.

There was some very dignified whooping from our row while Megs got up to go and stand on the stage. I thought the next two choices were very ill advised.

It made me feel a bit more hopeful about my own chances.

Next was 10NM.

When Miss R called out Icky's name someone near the back made a vomiting noise. I hadn't even paid them. It just goes to show that I'm clearly not the only one that thinks she is an evil pixie of pain, despair and stinky perfume.

'I feel sorry for any Year Sevens that misbehave on her watch,' Angharad whispered.

I nodded. 'They'd better be careful; it will be easy for her to infiltrate their ranks. She's exactly the same size as them.'

'But not as smart,' Lily said.

I discretely laughed my pants off.

By the time we got to our form, my heart was a tiny bit poundy.

The good thing about having a surname that starts with 'A' is that you get to know whether to thump someone or to do a star jump straight away.

'Faith Ashby,' Miss Ramsbottom said with a definite sneer.

I did a star jump. And then skipped up to the stage. I'm going to be a prefect! When I squeezed in next to Megs I waited for her heartfelt congratulations.

'You've still got Ang's jumper on your head,' she said.

I whipped the jumper off.

Miss R called out three more names from my tutor group. Angharad was one of them but Lily wasn't. To be honest, ever since she'd told me that she'd talked about her toe-sock collection in her interview I had been a bit concerned about her chances. I hoped she wasn't going to be upset. I peered between heads to where she was sat in the audience. She had her feet up on my seat and she seemed to be tying her shoelaces together.

I didn't think she was too upset.

By the time Miss R got to the end of her list there were about twenty of us up on stage.

Everybody clapped until Ramsbum waved her hands for quiet. 'Well done, girls. I'm pleased to say that the interview panel were very impressed with the calibre of the applicants this year and they assured me that there are a number of excellent candidates for the position of head girl.'

She pulled a face that didn't look at all pleased or assured.

'In the end they chose a young lady that they found to be intelligent, polite and with a proven track record of service to the school. They were also impressed by the amount of support that this girl had from the other interviewees. It gives me pleasure to announce that Westfield High's new head girl is ...' She paused in what I imagine she thought was a dramatic fashion. I promised myself that if Icky was made head I'd run away and join the circus.

'Angharad Jones,' Miss Ramsbottom said.

Angharad's eyes nearly popped out of her head. 'Me?' she said.

I gave her a hug.

There was some very loud clapping. Everyone loves Ang.

Except Icky. She was pouting and generally looking like a grumpy garden gnome.

Miss Ramsbottom clapped her hands for quiet. 'I'm sure that you will all assist these girls in doing their duty and ensuring that our school is one that we can all be proud of.'

That'll never happen. But everyone was so pleased and so end-of-termy that we gave Ramsbum a big clap too.

I'm so happy for Ang; she's going to be a brilliant head girl.

SATURDAY 21ST JULY

It was great waking up this morning knowing that I don't have to do anything until September. I might ask Mum if I can get a TV and a fridge in my room and then I'd only have to get out of bed when I wanted to see my friends.

When I came downstairs for breakfast Mum said, 'Granny's here.'

'Well, that's a relief. The one thing missing from my perfect day was the presence of someone so old they can't stand still too long for fear that once their joints stop moving they might never get going again.'

'She's got you a present.'

'I've always said a day without Granny is a day without sunshine.'

I pushed past Mum and into the sitting room. 'Where is she? Where's my favourite grandmother?'

Granny swivelled round in her chair and narrowed her beady eyes. 'I'm your only grandmother.'

I stared right back at her. 'Don't think I couldn't rustle up another grandparent if I thought you needed replacing.'

'I hear you've been working hard for your exams.'

It's nice to know that for once my parents are making conversation about something important, i.e. me, rather than waffling on about the price of dish cloths.

'And you're finished now, are you?'

'I am. In fact, before I start on my summer of rock and roll and Magnum ice creams, I might have time for a quick game of Scabby Queen with you.'

Granny nodded graciously as if she was doing me the favour.

After we'd had a few hands she pulled a small package out of her handbag. 'This is for you. To say thank you for your help with the flowers, and well done for working so hard for your exams.'

I opened the paper carefully in case it was five hundred pounds in notes – which is what I always ask for at Christmas and my birthday, but for some reason no one has ever run with that suggestion.

Inside was a jewellery box. I opened it and inside there was a pair of earrings. Teeny tiny, super sparkly earrings. Really sparkly. 'Those aren't . . . ?'

Granny looked pleased with herself. 'Diamonds? Yes, they are. Your mother said you wanted some.'

I made a mental note to tell Mum that I want a Mercedes and a studio apartment.

'Thank you Granny!' And then, I have to admit, I hugged her.

'You may as well have them now,' she said. 'Otherwise, you'll be trying to bump me off to get them in my will.'

I beamed at her. 'Granny, I can honestly say that right now, I fully intend to let you live out your natural life span with no foul play on my part.'

'I'll take that as another thank you. Of course, they're not my best ones.' She snapped her handbag closed. 'You'll have to prise those out of my cold dead hands.'

'Will do, Granny. Will do.'

LATER

As I was in such a good mood I had lunch with my family and let them know how much I love them. I said to Sam, 'Have you done something new with your hair? You look slightly less like a moron than usual.'

Sam stole one of my sandwiches and I gave him an affectionate throttling while I stole three back.

'And you two,' I said to Mum and Dad. 'You're both looking very young and energetic for a couple of old codgers.'

They're not a bad lot. I gave them all a hug before I headed out this afternoon.

And I didn't even pick anyone's pockets.

LATER STILL

Megs's dad dropped us off at the farm where the music festival was taking place. Three fields had been transformed into some kind of tent city. There were two music stages and loads of food sellers. Mostly of the veggie organic variety that my mum loves, which is fine except that a mushroom burger costs a packet (and when you ask for a plastic fork or a paper napkin they look at you as if you're trying to single-handedly destroy the planet). There were also tons of stalls selling everything from bangles to old vinyl records. We met the others and headed to the local bands stage because someone Westy knows was playing drums in the first band on.

They were one of those bands that mostly shout and thump their guitars, rather than going in for any of that melodic harmony stuff, but they weren't bad. By the time they'd finished, the field was starting to get crowded and I was roasting.

Westy looked like he was being boiled in his clothes. 'Phew! They were amazing weren't they? I can do that thing he did at the end when you put the drumstick between your teeth. Well, I can do it sometimes; by the time my band gets a gig I'll be really good at it.' He threw himself down on the crushed grass. 'Who's going to get me a drink?'

'I'll get everyone a drink,' I said and I completely promise that it was just to be kind, and to spend some of the money Dad gave me, and not because of what I said next, because I didn't even know that I was going to say what I said next. You know how my mouth just runs away. It opened up all by itself and said, 'Come and help me carry them,' to Ethan.

'Sure.' He stood up and pushed his curls out of his eyes while I tried to take a good long look at him without it seeming like I was staring.

The sun was really beating down and there were a lot of people milling about.

Ethan scanned the crowd. 'It's busy, isn't it?'

I wondered if he was looking for anyone in particular.

Then I spotted Dawn. She was stood on top of a hay bale to get a better look at the main stage where some folky band were playing. She was dressed all in black and didn't seem to be feeling the heat at all. She looked amazing. I had a horrible vision of Ethan spotting her and going over to chat and ... them getting friendly again. But rather than dragging him away, I said, 'Dawn's over there.' Because, let's face it, if a boy agrees to get in a queue for drinks with you, it only means something if he chooses to do it when he knows that his beautiful ex-girlfriend is by herself on a hay bale nearby.

'I know,' he said. 'I bumped into her at the gate.'

What I wanted to ask was, *What did she say? What did you say?* But I settled for, 'Did you?'

'Yeah, she had some terrible idea about the two of us hanging out, but I told her I was here with you.'

I wondered if that meant 'you' as in me, or 'you' as in you lot.

'So you're not bothered that she's here?'

Ethan shrugged. 'I can't stop people who've annoyed me a bit from going where they choose.'

'Although, obviously, in an ideal world that is exactly what we'd be able to do,' I said.

'I'll work on that when they come to their senses and make me king.'

I sneaked another look at him; he looked better than he had done in ages. 'So … does that mean Dawn didn't break your heart?'

'Nah, I mean before she made me look like a bit of an idiot I thought she was …'

'Gorgeous?'

'She was a good laugh. But to be honest, Faith, it wasn't exactly a surprise when I heard that she'd been seeing other people. She'd told me that she wanted to keep it casual. She said I could see other people if I wanted to.'

'Oh.' Imagine dating Ethan and not wanting him all to yourself.

'I was going try it, but when it came to it, I realised I'm not that sort of person.'

I was struggling a bit to take this all in. In spite of everything he'd said I couldn't help wondering if he would still be with Dawn if she'd shown a bit more commitment. It wasn't a very nice thought.

I bought eight cans of Coke and we went back to the others.

The rest of the afternoon was pretty good; we ate chips and listened to the music. Lily had her face painted and Westy ate so many burgers that Angharad finally got to use the emergency indigestion pill that she carries around with her. But I was slightly distracted thinking about Ethan.

I waited until the others were engrossed in

watching Westy try to persuade the man running the kids' bouncy castle that he should let him have a go, then I sidled up to Ethan. 'Can I ask you something?'

His face spread into a lazy grin. 'Anything.'

'That time in the ghost train . . .'

His grin disappeared. 'Are you thinking that I'm a horrible hypocrite because I didn't want Dawn to see other people, but there I was putting my arm around you in the dark?'

Which was a good point. As if things weren't complicated enough already.

'Actually, I wasn't thinking you were a horrible hypocrite, but thanks for suggesting it because now I come to think about it, it was hypocritical. Wasn't it?'

He looked at the ground. 'I . . . Dawn said she didn't mind.'

'What if I minded? You were just using me to see if you wanted to do this whole casual relationship thing.'

'Is that what you think?'

That didn't seem like a fair question.

'What am I supposed to think?'

'Faith!' Westy grabbed me by the shoulder. 'Faith, you've got to tell this bloke that inside my manly body is the heart of a child! He says I'm too old for the bouncy castle.'

'Sorry, Westy. I'm ... I've got a bit of a headache. I think I'm going to sit in the shade for a while.'

I turned to leave but Megs caught my arm and gave me an enquiring look.

'I'm fine,' I said. 'I just need to cool down for ten minutes.'

So I walked off to the edge of the field and sat down under a tree with my back to the crowds. I wasn't sure if I was being daft or not. I just felt a bit hurt. It seemed like the only reason Ethan had even thought about kissing me was to play Dawn at her own game.

'Oh, it's you.'

I looked up to find Icky and someone who I assumed must be her latest boyfriend. He had that look in his eyes; you know, the look of someone who's been hit around the head with a cricket bat until they agreed to a date with a girl who I can only imagine came about as the result of an ill-thought out experiment to splice the heart of a troll into the body of a pig.

Icky looked down her snout at me. 'I should have known. You're the only person sad enough to come to a music festival by yourself.'

I really wasn't in the mood for this so I stood up. 'I'm not by myself! My friends are over there.'

She smirked. 'Of course they are. Do they always make you sit in the next field?'

I looked at the boy. He was shifting uncomfortably.

'Bet you didn't know she was such a charmer, huh?'

He turned to Icky, but didn't quite manage to look her in the eye. 'Actually, Vicky, I'm just going to go and find Dan.'

And he was gone.

I beamed at Icky. 'Wow. He didn't last long, did he? Either you're going to have to start dating boys who don't mind your nasty remarks, or you're going to have to learn to keep up the pretence that you're not an evil, rat-toothed, imbecilic, stinking, pig-troll for a little longer.'

'At least I've got a boyfriend.'

'Yeah, we'll see. Anyway, Vicks, it's been a blast but I expect you've got pig-troll business to do, so off you go. It's over there.'

She turned round to look. 'What is?'

'The burger stall.'

'Why would I want to go over there?'

'I thought you might need the condiments. Bit of ketchup, maybe a drop of mustard.'

She put her hands on her hips. 'What the hell are you talking about?'

'Your head. I can't imagine anyone could possibly chomp that down without a bit of sauce. After all, it's mostly fat and gristle, isn't it?'

'What?'

'Remember? You said if one of my lot got to be head girl that you would eat your own head. And Angharad has been officially appointed.'

She shook her fatty gristle head. 'You're ridiculous.'

'Hmm, maybe. The thing is, Angharad is one of my very best friends. Which means that if I have a ridiculous idea about how you should be the prefect in charge of litter duty or the Year Nine bus queue, then I think Angharad will listen to me, don't you?'

She narrowed her hard little eyes. 'You are such a b—'

'Brilliant predictor of an accurate future?' someone interrupted.

I knew it was Ethan, even before I turned round. He was stood right next to us holding an ice cream. I've got no idea how long he'd been listening for.

'No, she's a lit—'

'A little diamond,' Ethan interrupted again.

Icky looked between the two of us. 'You're both completely—'

'Awesome!' Ethan and I said together.

Icky gave one oink-roar of frustration and stropped off.

Serves her right.

There was a pause.

Ethan held out the ice cream.

'I bought you this. I thought it might help you cool down.'

'I don't want it.'

'Oh.' He looked at the ice cream and then around the field and I knew he was looking for a bin.

Suddenly, I was cross with him again. 'There's no need to throw it away! There's no point in letting it go to waste.' I reached out and took it from him. 'What are you? Some kind of moron?'

'Apparently so.' He looked a bit upset and I was glad because at least that meant he cared what I think about him.

But that didn't let him off the hook. 'Yeah, well, no one likes feeling that they're someone's failed experiment and I—'

'Faith, listen to me.'

'I don't want to listen to you.'

'But you've got to. Stop talking and eat your ice cream.'

I took a lick or seven. Just so it didn't melt everywhere.

'Faith, this isn't about Dawn, I don't care about Dawn. It's about you.'

Which is a sentence I usually enjoy hearing, but I still wasn't satisfied. 'But ... the ghost train, you said it was because Dawn said—'

'I wanted to kiss you in the ghost train because I've always wanted to kiss you.'

I froze. He wanted to kiss me.

'I wanted to kiss you during choir rehearsals, at the playground, at your birthday party. That time Cam threw vegetable soup over us; there isn't a single location in this town that I haven't thought about kissing you in.'

I couldn't believe I was hearing this. A little seed of happiness was sprouting inside me, but things still didn't quite make sense. 'But you *didn't* kiss me in the ghost train because you liked Dawn.'

'No.' He said it so firmly that a girl walking past turned around to look at him. Ethan didn't notice, his eyes were fixed on me. 'No, that's not what happened.' He took a step closer to me and my heart squeezed hard. 'I didn't kiss you then because I liked you too much. I didn't want things to be like that between us. I wanted it to be special and I wanted it to be just about us. Nobody else.'

This was amazing. And yet I was distracted by a small voice in my head cursing me for ever accepting that stupid ice cream. Ethan was finally saying the words I'd waited so long to hear, and all I could do was worry about drips. Something really important was happening here. He had said 'us' like that was a thing. I risked a look at him.

His dark eyes were watching me, large and earnest. He took a deep breath. 'I split up with Dawn because I wanted to be with you. I didn't think that was going to happen because you always seemed to be interested in someone else, but I still had to split up with her because I didn't want to be with anyone who wasn't you.'

Oh wow. I swallowed. 'But ... you were so cross with me when you found out I knew about Dawn and that boy in McDonalds.'

He sighed. 'I was hurt that you didn't say anything about it. I mean, I thought that we were good enough friends to look out for each other.'

So he wasn't upset that Dawn had kissed another boy. He was upset that I didn't tell him. It was time for me to do some straight talking. 'I was afraid to say anything. I didn't want you to think I was jealous of Dawn – even though I was. I didn't want you to hate me.'

He leaned in towards me. 'I am so far from hating you.'

I'd waited a long time for those words. (Actually I thought the words 'princess of my heart' might be in there somewhere, but I wasn't going to quibble.) And somehow, instead of looking irresistibly snoggable, which is what I'd always planned to do in this situation, I ended up snorting out a half laugh.

He blinked.

'Sorry!' I said. 'I'm not really laughing. It's just, you know, weird, us being so serious. I keep expecting you to crack a joke.'

His face fell a bit and I cursed myself for not being able to keep it together.

'Is that what you think of me, Faith?' he asked. 'That I'm just some fast-talking show off?'

'No, of course not. Being a fast-talking show off is only one of the many qualities that attracts me to you.'

His eyes sparked when I said that.

'Do you know what? I find it pretty easy to shoot my mouth off. If you ask any of my teachers they'll tell you that I've always got a smart answer for everything, but I've been struggling for a long time to find the words to tell you what I want to say. The truth is that I don't have a brilliantly clever speech prepared; I just want to tell you the truth. I like you, Faith.' He looked right into my eyes. 'I really like you.'

He likes me.

I focused on making my mouth talk. 'I like you too.'

Slowly, he reached out and took hold of my left hand, which was the one not holding a dripping ice cream.

I couldn't move. I couldn't breathe.

He lifted my hand to his lips and kissed the inside of my wrist.

I've got no idea how I was managing to remain upright at this point because it felt like my whole body was pretty busy with the fireworks going off inside me.

I looked at him. With his lovely curly hair and his lovely sneery mouth and his clever clever eyes.

He looked back at me and his eyes were saying it again, saying that he liked me. My stomach swooped like it does when you're on a swing and all I could think about was how amazing he is.

And then I did something I never thought I'd do.

I dropped a perfectly good ice cream on the ground.

And I kissed Ethan.

It was like walking into an electric fence of happiness. My whole body was fizzing with joy.

When we stopped to breathe a bit. He kept his arms around me and he said, 'Do you know how long I've been waiting to do that?'

I shook my head.

'Since the minute I met you. Remember? You laid into Vicky with a particularly vicious and hilarious put-down, and I thought to myself, that's the sweet-natured girl for me.'

'It's nice that you like me for my cutting remarks as well as my amazing good looks.'

'Don't forget your upright moral character.'

We cracked up.

Then I caught his eye again and we stopped still. My mouth was about an inch from his. He smelled like clean t-shirts; fresh and cottony. He's got a chickenpox scar in his hairline.

We kissed again.

'Wayhay!' someone bellowed behind us.

We broke apart and saw that it was Cam. He ruffled Ethan's hair. 'Finally!' he said.

The others were right behind. I looked at Westy to see if he seemed upset, but he was beaming. He's all Skype-snoggy with Josette now, anyway.

My eyes found Megs who gave me a huge grin. 'You lot owe me money,' she said to the others.

Unbelievable. There I was getting together with my dream boy at last and Megs was thinking about her ill-gotten gains. 'Were you betting on us?' I asked. 'Does that mean the rest of you didn't think we'd get together?' I was slightly annoyed; surely they could all see what a brilliant couple Ethan and I are.

'No, we all knew it would happen,' Lily said.

'They said it would happen sooner,' Megs interrupted. 'I was the only one confident in your ability to faff about and muck things up for several months.'

I tried to glare at her, but I was just so happy I could only manage to say, 'You'd better split that cash with me.'

Ethan still had an arm around me and we stayed like that while we all walked up the hill to find a patch of grass big enough for us all to sit down.

The sun was going down.

Someone was playing the violin and leaping about on the main stage.

Ethan turned to look at me and asked, 'Will you be my girlfriend?'

He said it so seriously that I didn't even make a joke. I just said, 'Yes.' And grinned like a maniac. I was already feeling pretty good but once he'd said that, my insides really went to town and started whirling and fluttering about. This wasn't just fireworks; it was a full on internal Disneyland parade.

Ethan squeezed my hand. 'Let me just be completely clear about this: my totally exclusive, doesn't snog anyone else and wears a t-shirt with a picture of me on it at all times, girlfriend?'

The Mickey Mouse in my tummy did a triple backflip and punched the air. 'Yes to the first two bits. And you?'

'Definitely. I'll even wear the t-shirt.'

'What, with a picture of yourself on?'

'I don't think you'll be surprised to hear that I have already got several printed. You never know when someone will ask me to be president.'

I laughed.

He laughed too.

And he gave me a look and I knew what it meant. *This is going to be brilliant. We're going to hang* out together and say sarcastic stuff and wind up Icky and tease our mates and kiss and eat pizza and go to the park and kiss some more and talk and talk and talk. We're going to have the best time.

The sunset was turning the sky pink.

There are so many good things in my life. I know I'm not perfect and I know life isn't perfect. But sitting there, in the warm evening with all my mates, and my new boyfriend holding my hand, it was a completely perfect moment.

And I know there are going to be a lot more.